Lightning Strikes

Ahead, the wall of clouds ripped apart as the sea foamed like the mouth of a rabid dog. Thunder exploded in deafening claps, and I was nearly blinded by dazzling flashes of lightning. Lightning bolts crossed one another, hurled from every side. In their path, waves rose up toward us like fire-breathing monsters.

READ ALL THE BOOKS
IN THE **wishbone** *classics* SERIES:

Wishbone classics

A Journey to the Center of the Earth

retold by Billy Aronson

Interior illustrations by

Joe Boddy

Wishbone illustrations by

Kathryn Yingling

HarperPaperbacks

A Division of HarperCollins*Publishers*

HarperPaperbacks *A Division of* HarperCollins*Publishers*
10 East 53rd Street, New York, N.Y. 10022

Cover photographs by Carol Kaelson

A Creative Media Applications Production
Art Direction by Fabia Wargin Design
Production by Alan Barnett, Inc.

First printing: November 1996

Printed in the United States of America

HarperPaperbacks and colophon are trademarks of HarperCollins*Publishers*
WISHBONE is a trademark and service mark of Big Feats! Entertainment

❖ 10 9 8 7 6 5 4 3

PROFESSOR LIDENBROCK

Introduction

All set to enter a world of action, adventure, drama, and laughs? Then come along with me, Wishbone. You may have seen me on my TV show. Often I am the main character and sometimes I am the sidekick, but I'm always right in the middle of a thrilling story. Now, I'm going to be your guide as we explore one of the world's greatest books — A JOURNEY TO THE CENTER OF THE EARTH. Together we'll meet a lot of interesting characters and discover places we've never been! I guarantee lots of surprises too! So find a nice comfy chair, and get ready to read with **Wishbone**.

Table of Contents

Jules Verne

Jules Verne grew up in the early 1800s in a French seaport called Nantes. When he was ten, Jules sneaked onto a ship bound for the West Indies, eager for a life of travel and adventure. But before the ship left for the open seas, his father caught him, dragged him off the ship, and sent him to his room. Jules promised his father that he would never again run away in search of adventure; he would take incredible journeys only in his imagination.

When he grew up, the place Verne wanted to let his imagination run wild was in the theater. Although Verne had gone to law school, he really wanted to be a playwright, not a lawyer. Since he couldn't get anyone to perform his plays, Verne took all kinds of jobs to support himself. He worked as a teacher, a banker, and an actor. Sometimes he wrote articles about science for kids' magazines.

One day Verne read about a scientist who was going to attempt to take a trip in a box carried by a huge balloon. Verne was so impressed, he decided to write an article about what this historic trip might be like.

Editors at fifteen different magazines rejected the article. But one of those editors suggested that Verne try writing the story not as fact, but as fiction.

Thrilled by this suggestion, Verne wrote a story about a scientist who took an amazing journey in a balloon, flying all the way down the world's longest river, the Nile, to discover its source. *Five Weeks in a Balloon* was its title, and it became an instant best seller. Verne had done more than write a great story. With this book, he had created a whole new kind of story: fiction based on science.

Verne went on to write almost a hundred science fiction books, many of which involved incredible journeys. The most famous of these include *Twenty Thousand Leagues Under the Sea, Around the World in Eighty Days, and A Journey to the Center of the Earth.* Though Verne wrote in French, you will have no trouble finding English translations in your library. In fact, Verne's books have been translated into 104 languages!

The tradition of science fiction writing begun by Verne's books is popular to this day. These stories also paved the way for our sci-fi TV shows, movies, comics, and even artwork.

Some of the ideas in Verne's books even led to great scientific works. Countless scientists have given Jules Verne credit for pointing them to important discoveries, inventions, and historic journeys.

So brace yourself. The book you are about to read may inspire you to see the world in a whole new way...and even to change it.

ABOUT
A JOURNEY TO THE CENTER OF THE EARTH

Hey there, reader! It's me, Wishbone, telling you to pack your bags, because— YOU ARE ABOUT TO SET OUT ON A REMARKABLE JOURNEY.

It's not a bike ride, a plane ride, or a quick run through the woods on all fours. Sure, you can go pretty far pretty fast on those types of journeys and see some exciting things along the way. But on the journey you're about to take in this story, you're going to travel at fantastic speeds to places no one has ever been—and you'll see sights no one has ever seen.

You can do these incredible things because you'll be using the most powerful vehicle of all: your own imagination. (So you won't need your bags. A comfy chair and a lamp will do.)

Every time you read a work of fiction, your imagination takes you for a ride. (Fiction is a story that someone made up, as opposed to a story based on something that really happened, which is called non-fiction.) This journey of the imagination involves a special kind of fiction called science fiction.

In science fiction, the writer uses science as a springboard for a story. Sometimes the writer uses scientific laws that have been proven and tested. Sometimes the writer makes up laws that he or she wishes were true or that might be proven true someday. In either case, the story is based on real or imagined science.

Reading science fiction gives you a feeling that's very different from the feeling you get while reading other kinds of fiction, such as fairy tales. When you read a fairy tale about goblins, fairy godmothers, or talking wolves, you realize that the events could never really happen. But science fiction can be exciting and chilling; you get the feeling that the incredible things you're reading about might someday, somewhere, just maybe...really happen! Because the amazing events are based on science, they feel unbelievable and believable at the same time!

Writing good science fiction is hard. Besides being able to tell a good story, the writer has to appreciate science. In this science fiction journey, you're in great hands. The writer is none other than the man who created serious science fiction! That's right, he's the father of science fiction—Jules Verne.

MAIN CHARACTERS

Professor Lidenbrock: A professor of geology.

Axel: Professor Lidenbrock's nephew and also a scientist.

Martha: Professor Lidenbrock's cook.

Gretchen: Axel's fiancée.

Mr. Fridriksson: A professor and friend of Lidenbrock's.

Hans: A duckhunter who also serves as a guide.

SETTING

Like Jules Verne himself, the main characters in *A Journey to the Center of the Earth* lived in Europe in the 1800s. At that time, people all over Europe and America were becoming more curious about science.

One scientific discovery after another brought about an avalanche of change. The new steam engine gave people a whole new way to get around. Automobiles and airplanes were being developed. So were electric lights and telephones. Deep in the earth, fossils were being found that helped people understand how the human race began. In space, new planets were being discovered. People loved to learn about these new discoveries and to imagine where they might lead.

Many scientists tried bold experiments and took daring journeys, hoping to expand the boundaries of knowledge. And many readers searched for books that would expand their minds...books that would thrill them with clues about what was possible...books such as *A Journey to the Center of the Earth!*

1

The Mysterious Note

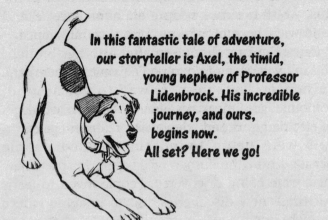

In this fantastic tale of adventure,
our storyteller is Axel, the timid,
young nephew of Professor
Lidenbrock. His incredible
journey, and ours,
begins now.
All set? Here we go!

Looking back on everything that happened, I can hardly believe it wasn't all a dream! Even now, I'm amazed when I remember the incredible adventure that began on that fateful day.

The day I'm talking about, of course, is the day my uncle got the idea for our historic journey. My uncle, better known as Professor Lidenbrock, was a famous professor of geology—the science that deals with how the earth was formed and what it's made of. One of the finest geologists of the day, my uncle had analyzed hundreds of different types of rocks and shared his findings with great scientists around the world. Since I, too, was interested in geology, I had come to live with my uncle at his home in Hamburg,

Germany. There we could study and discover, day after day.

On this particular morning, I was examining rocks in my uncle's laboratory as he did research in his library upstairs. At lunchtime, I headed to the kitchen, where our cook had set out a fine meal. But just as I was about to take my first slurp of soup, I was interrupted by a shriek from upstairs.

"Axel! Axel!" my uncle cried, "Come up here at once! Hurry up!"

When I got up to my uncle's library, he was holding a large, dusty book with yellowed pages.

Taking no notice of me, my uncle just stood there, staring into the volume. Then he began tapping his forehead and muttering to himself, "Wonderful! Wonderful!"

Normally, I'm very interested in my uncle's findings. But at this moment, I was much more interested in the bowl of soup waiting for me in the kitchen. **Axel is my kind of storyteller. The tale just started and he's already talking about food.**

When my uncle finally put down the volume, I realized that it wasn't the book itself he had been studying. It was a small, crinkled note he had found between the pages.

"Runic, my boy," he said, referring to the strange lettering that covered the note, "a language with an unusual alphabet, used in Iceland, Finland, and Germany between the fourth and fourteenth centuries."

Though my uncle understood dozens of different languages, he knew as many letters of the runic alphabet as I did: none. But he wasn't going to let that stop him from reading that ancient scribble. In a flash, he climbed onto a stepladder, yanked his trusty runic dictionary from the bookshelves, and began trying to translate the message.

I stood there as patiently as I could as he began to translate. How I hoped his stomach would cry out to him, as mine was crying out to me! **Oooh! Mine is crying out too!** But I had no such luck. When the clock struck two, the cook called up to remind us that lunch was getting quite cold. "Who needs lunch!" replied my uncle, without even lifting his eyes from his book.

For the next three minutes, my love of politeness battled with my love of food. Finally, the love of food won out. I charged downstairs and devoured my soup (not minding that it was cold), as well as a ham omelet and two helpings of stew— before rinsing off an apple for dessert.

I can relate to Axel. When you've got to eat, you've got to eat!

As I was finishing the apple I heard my uncle call my name so loudly that I nearly sprang up the stairs in a single leap. "It's in code!" he declared. "These letters are

17

indeed runic, I'm sure of that. But they don't spell any particular words. They must be in code. It must be some sort of secret message!"

I was about to ask whether the "message" might not just be a lot of nonsense, when my uncle handed me a pen. "Sit down," he commanded. "Write these letters as I dictate to you."

One at a time, he translated from the runic as I wrote down the odd string of letters:

SLEFFENSFORETARCEHTOTNIOG
SEHCUOTSIRATRACSFOWODAHSEHTEREHW
HTRAEEHTFORETNECEHTHCAERLLIWUOYDNA
MMESSUNKASENRATIDIDI

"A coded message, as sure as I live and breathe!" he exclaimed.

"But from whom?" he asked. "The book was written in the twelfth century. But the paper on which the note is written isn't nearly as old as the pages of the book. So the note certainly is not from the person who wrote the book, but from someone who owned it."

With that, my uncle flipped to the inside front cover of the book, where he found, written in tiny letters, a name that made him gasp. "Arne Saknussemm!"

"Who?" I asked.

"Arne Saknussemm!" my uncle cried again. "The great sixteenth century Icelandic explorer! The note must have been written by him! I'm positive it contains news of a discovery made by the Great Saknussemm himself!"

"It might," I said, "but why would an explorer write a discovery in code? Wouldn't he want the world to know what he'd found? Why would he go to such trouble to keep it a secret?"

"How should I know?" answered my uncle, pacing wildly around the room. "But until I figure out what this note says, I will neither eat nor sleep." **No eating or sleeping? I'm going to have a serious talk with this guy.**

"But Uncle—" I began.

"And neither will you!" he added.

I suddenly felt lucky that I'd had an extra helping of stew at lunch. "Let's see," he muttered, studying the letters. "There are forty vowels...sixty-nine consonants...Nothing unusual about that. This phrase on the bottom row of letters looks strangely familiar...'TIDIDI.' Could that be the name of a tropical island somewhere? And look here! In the row above it! The word 'FOR'! But 'for' what, I wonder. 'FOR RET'? 'FOR RETNE'? 'FOR RETNECE'? Very challenging indeed, aye Axel?"

What was challenging to my uncle was becoming downright boring to me. My mind had already wandered to thoughts of his goddaughter, Gretchen, to whom I was engaged to be married. My dear Gretchen had been away on vacation and was due back within the hour. How I longed to see her smile again. How I longed to see anything outside the walls of this library, where my uncle was keeping me prisoner!

"Let's try it this way," my uncle barked. He wrote quickly, copying the letters onto another piece of paper. As he copied he arranged the horizontal rows of letters into vertical columns. Then he stood, stared at this new version of the message, and suddenly exclaimed, "Nothing! Still nothing!" He struck the table with his fist, darted out of the room and right out of the house.

2
A Backwards Invitation

Axel is about to make an amazing discovery…and wishes he hadn't!

"Isn't the master ever going to have his lunch?" asked the cook.

"Definitely not," I answered. "In fact, you can probably forget about dinner. He won't eat again, and neither will I, until he can figure out the meaning of some ridiculous note."

"You'll starve," she said.

I agreed with her and returned to the lab. What a relief it was to get back to my beloved rocks. It was more pleasant to examine my old stony friends than those strange letters.

As I worked, I couldn't help thinking about my poor uncle. I figured that he must be running up and down the road with the note pressed to his nose—or standing in the middle of a public square, gesturing wildly while babbling to himself. Would he hit upon a clue? Would he come home in a better mood? Would we ever eat again?

At one point, I took a break to examine the note. I tried grouping the letters in twos. Then threes. Then fours. I saw the words "SIR" and "TO" and "RAT" in there. Could this be a message about a "sir somebody" who did something amazing to a rat? I was getting nowhere.

After hours of trying to make sense of the note, my brain was on fire. My eyes were strained. The letters seemed to swirl around on the paper and dance before my eyes. To cool myself down, I started to fan myself with the note.

And then I saw it.

As I waved the note before my eyes I saw the paper from behind. As I looked through the paper from the back I saw the letters backwards—and recognized words! Clear, simple words! Words that fit together in sentences! I had broken the code! All you had to do to figure out the message was read it backwards!

I was thrilled by my discovery. But when I began to decode the message, my joy turned to horror. What a terrible secret I had read. A man had really dared to do that?

"Never!" I cried, jumping up. "I will never let my uncle know this secret. For nothing could stop him from taking this deadly journey. He'd make me go with him. We'd be lost forever. My dear uncle is nearly insane with curiosity already. The secret contained in this note would push him over the edge! He must never crack the code."

But what does it say? WHAT DOES IT SAY?

Just then, he came charging in, deep in thought. Some new way of trying to crack the code had entered his mind. He sat down with the note and began writing numbers above the letters. Then, on a separate piece of paper, he added the numbers together in different combinations. I realized his method couldn't possibly lead him to the secret. There was only one correct way to break the code. But still, I trembled as he stared at the note. Surely he'd stumble onto the secret any second!

Hours passed. My uncle paced, struggled, and pondered. The sun set. The town became quiet. And still my uncle worked away. *It's only a matter of time,* I thought to myself, as I fell asleep on the sofa.

But when I awoke in the morning, the poor man was still slaving away. He rubbed his bloodshot eyes as he muttered and scribbled and strained. I knew that a word from me could put an end to his suffering. But I refused to say it.

As the hours passed, two things weakened my determination to keep the secret: pity for my uncle and pity for my stomach. I wanted breakfast, but there was no way of getting it until the puzzle was solved. When I crept downstairs to sneak a pastry, I learned from the cook that there was none left. In fact, we were down to our last piece of bread. My uncle had left the front door locked, so the cook couldn't go food shopping! We were doomed!

As lunchtime came and went, my determination began to crumble. *Would it really be so awful to let my uncle know the secret?* I wondered. *There will be plenty of time to talk him out of making that ridiculous journey.*

And even if he does go, I'll be able to think up some excuse so I won't have to join him. Besides, he's going to figure out the message himself sooner or later. In the meantime, why should the cook and I starve?

When my uncle got up to go, I decided it was time to end my silence.

"Can I say something about the key?" I asked.

"The key to the front door?" he retorted.

"No," I replied. "The key."

He stopped dead in his tracks. He glanced at me from under his spectacles. Then he charged across the room and grabbed me by the shoulders.

"You don't mean…?" he asked, to which I simply nodded.

For a moment neither of us spoke.

"Look at the note again, just as it's written," I urged him. "But it doesn't mean a thing!" was his gruff answer.

"Not if read from left to right," I explained. "But when read from right to left—"

Snatching up the document, he read it backwards and read aloud:

GO INTO THE CRATER OF SNEFFELS WHERE THE SHADOW OF SCARTARIS TOUCHES AND YOU WILL REACH THE CENTER OF THE EARTH
I DID IT ARNE SAKNUSSEMM

My uncle leaped three feet into the air. **Not a bad trick for somebody with only two legs!** He ran around the room, delighted. He knocked over tables and chairs. He threw papers into the air. He fell into his armchair. Then, after catching his breath, he spoke: "Let's pack our suitcases at once, my boy!"

I began to get up my courage to talk my uncle out of this trip. The very idea of going to the center of the earth seemed completely insane. Although I hated getting him angry, I would have to speak up.

In the meantime, his anger was directed at the cook. "How could you let us run out of groceries?" he shouted. When I explained that he had locked us all in, he apologized and gave her the key. Later, while the cook shopped and then prepared lunch, my uncle packed his bag, humming happily to himself.

"Axel," he said as we ate, "you have done me a great service. Without you, this tremendous discovery would never have been made. So I'll see to it that you get to share the glory. That's right, my boy—you shall come with me on this historic trip."

I wanted to tell him how little interest I had in glory, but he continued. "Now, no matter what, you mustn't tell a soul about our plans," he directed me. "We must be the very first to follow in the Great Saknussemm's footsteps!"

"Who else would want to?" I replied softly.

"Scientists from around the world!" he answered. "They would be lining up to make the trip if they found out about this note!"

"But couldn't it be a prank?" I asked. "After all, whoever heard of places called 'Sneffels' or 'Scartaris'? To me, they sound like names made up by a practical joker."

My uncle chewed in silence for a moment. Then he took my hand and led me upstairs to his library. There, he opened an atlas to a large map of Iceland. He pointed out a mountain labeled "Sneffels." He explained that Sneffels was once an active volcano and that there was a crater on top of Sneffels that long ago served as its mouth. Then he pointed out another mountain next to Sneffels, which was labeled "Scartaris."

So there it was, the entire meaning of that awful message: The shadow of Scartaris points out a certain path into Mount Sneffels. A person who enters that crater and follows that path could, the note promised, reach the very center of the earth. If only my uncle were not so determined that the "someone" should be us!

They're going to try to get to the center of the earth? This journey sounds like a dog's dream come true! I mean, I've dug a few feet into the ground to bury bones—even a few yards. But to go miles and miles below where any bone has ever been buried ...below where anyone has ever gone... It would be dark. It would be scary. It would be incredible!

3
Horrifying First Steps

While Professor Lidenbrock is making hasty preparations for the journey, Axel is looking for excuses to stay home. Let's see if he succeeds.

I was just beginning to pack my bag when a word my uncle had spoken exploded in my brain. In a flash, I was in his room.

"Did you say Sneffels is a volcano?" I asked. "How do you know it won't erupt when we're climbing into its mouth?"

"Dear Axel," he assured me, "Sneffels hasn't erupted since 1229. A volcano that has been silent for six hundred years is no more likely to spit lava into the sky than you or I!"

As I watched him pack, another fear filled my mind. "What about the theory that the inside of the Earth is thousands of degrees hot? Surely, we'd burn up as we approached it!" I said.

The theory Axel is referring to is called the Theory of Central Heat. According to this theory, the center of the earth is extremely hot. Scientists first got this idea when they noticed that lava is boiling hot

when it shoots out of the mouth of a volcano. Today we know that the Theory of Central Heat is true; it's thousands of degrees hot, deep in the earth!

"Nonsense," he replied. "Yes, lava is hot when it reaches the surface of the earth. But it's not hot because the inside of the earth is hot. It's hot because of friction! As it rushes upward the lava rubs against rock and becomes hot—just as your two hands become warm when you rub them together quickly. The inside of the earth is no hotter than the outside. I'm sure of it."

There was no reasoning with the man. He would believe any theory that supported his decision to go—and ignore any theory that didn't.

I began to feel that I was being led by a madman. So I went to visit the one person who could talk me out of following him to my death—Gretchen.

After hugging her hello, I told her everything. In great detail, I explained the horrifying trip on which my uncle wanted to take me. How disappointed I was by her response!

"What a fabulous journey!" she exclaimed. "How I wish I were a geologist so I could go too. What an honor it will be to accompany Professor Lidenbrock on this historic trip."

"But dear Gretchen," I answered, "I thought you would be the first to speak out against this crazy business!"

"Just the opposite," she answered. "I'm so proud of what you're doing. I can't wait to hear all about it when you return!"

That did it. Now I had no choice.

When I got home, my uncle was in the yard laying out ropes, tools, and torches. "Where have you been wasting your time?" he asked me. "Hurry up and get packing, my boy. We leave first thing in the morning!"

When my uncle said "first thing," he meant it. At five the next morning, we were off. **Five in the morning? Oh, way too early for this little dog.**

We took one train and then another and then another as we made our way north across Germany. My uncle was so deep in his thoughts that he hardly said a word—except when there was a delay of any kind. Then he would rage, pace, and mutter until we were back on our way.

Finally, we crossed the border into Denmark and arrived in its capital city of Copenhagen. From there we made our way to the docks, to take a boat to Iceland. How relieved I was to learn that no boat would leave for Iceland that day. How I hoped no boat ever would! But once again, my hopes were crushed. A little schooner, the Valkyrie, was scheduled to leave for Iceland on June 2—less than a week away.

In the meantime, my uncle and I took time for some sightseeing. We were surrounded by magnificent palaces, beautiful bridges, and incredible castles. Nothing seemed to interest my uncle except a tall steeple he spotted on the horizon. "That way!"

he commanded.

When we arrived at the church, I was puzzled. It wasn't nearly as beautiful as the other buildings we'd seen. Except for its tall steeple, with its countless winding stairs, there was nothing special about the old church at all.

But it was exactly this steeple that interested my uncle. "Let's climb, my boy," he said.

"But I never climb church towers," I answered. "I get dizzy in high places."

"That's just why you must climb this one," he insisted. "Your dizziness must be cured."

With a groan, I followed his order and climbed. My uncle hurried up, leading the way. After a few dozen steps, my head began to swim. After about a hundred and fifty steps, I felt the air getting colder. I looked up at the sky—and grabbed the railing and nearly fainted.

"Don't stop now, Axel!" cried my uncle.

"I can't go any farther, Uncle," I told him.

"Up, I say!" he commanded.

I kept on climbing, even though my whole body trembled more and more with every step. The sky and earth all seemed to swirl together. The steeple seemed to be a rocket ship rushing through space. My legs gave way. I began to crawl on my hands and knees. Finally, I closed my eyes as my uncle dragged me up the last few steps.

"Look around you!" he said. "In our journey to the center of the earth, you may have to look down into a deep pit at some point. This is good practice."

Slowly, shivering, I opened my eyes. First I saw the cold, fluffy clouds through which we seemed to float. Far away I could see the castles of Copenhagen, the grassy plains surrounding the town, and the sea. Fearful as I was, I rose to my feet to take in this tremendous view.

When we finally returned to the ground, I fell

to my knees and kissed the pavement. "That's enough for today," said my uncle. "Tomorrow we'll repeat the lesson."

And so we did—day after day for five days.

Sounds like Axel did some pretty serious training. If this is a preview of things to come, his summer isn't going to be much of a vacation!

4
All Our Ducks in a Row

Finally Tuesday came, and it was time for the schooner, *Valkyrie* to depart. As our little boat rocked up and down across the waves my poor uncle became seasick. He spent the whole trip throwing up over the side of the boat!

But even in his pain, he stood in amazement at one point as we neared Iceland. He caught sight of a huge mountain on the horizon, and gasped. "Behold!" he cried. "Behold Mount Sneffels!"

Though the mountain was visible, it was still many miles away from Reykjavik, the town at which we docked. Before beginning our trek across Iceland to the mountain, we dropped in on a scientist friend of my uncle's, a man named Fridriksson, to spend the night.

At dinner my uncle tried to get information about Saknussemm from our host—without letting him know what we were up to. "I'm curious," my uncle began, "whether your library has any books about a certain Icelandic explorer. I believe he was called Sackmuffin, or something like that."

Lidenbrock doesn't want to let Fridriksson know about the journey he's planning, since he doesn't want competition. So when he asks about Saknussemm and Mount Sneffels, he has to play dumb. I've been asked to play dead, but never to play dumb.

"Arne Saknussemm!" our host cried. "One of the greatest explorers of his day or any other!"

"That's him," replied my uncle.

"A brave and brilliant man," Mister Fridriksson continued, "and from right here in Iceland!"

"Yes, yes," my uncle said, "but do they have any books by him?"

"There are none," was our host's answer.

"None in Iceland?" my uncle asked.

"None anywhere," Mister Fridriksson explained. "The rulers of his day found Saknussemm's ideas insane. So they gathered his books, burned them all, and forbade him to write any more."

My uncle could hardly hide his excitement. "That explains the secret note!" he blurted.

"Secret note?" asked our host. "Have you come upon some precious find, Lidenbrock?"

"Oh no, no, no, no," my uncle stuttered. "I was just remembering a grocery list...I couldn't read the handwriting...never mind."

After a few minutes more, the conversation took a rather lucky turn. Mister Fridriksson said, "I hope that while you're visiting Iceland, you'll get a chance to explore our extraordinary mountains."

"Should I really bother?" my uncle asked slyly. "After all, I'm sure all the great mountains have been explored already, haven't they?"

"Not really," said Mister Fridriksson. "Actually, it's amazing how many unknown volcanoes have hardly been studied. Like that one you can see on the horizon—Mount Sneffels."

My uncle squeezed his knees together to keep

himself from jumping for joy. "Maybe you're right," he said. "As long as I'm here, maybe I will have a look at Mount—Sniffles? Snaffles?"

"Sneffels," said our host, completely fooled by my uncle's act. "Unfortunately, I'm too busy to join you. But you will need someone to help you find your way across the marshy terrain between here and Sneffels. And I know just the man."

When I awoke the next morning, I found my uncle speaking with the man who would be our guide. Hans, as he was called, appeared to be almost seven feet tall. With his arms bulging with muscles, the man reminded me of Hercules! His long blond hair hung down almost to his powerful shoulders.

How calm he appeared to be! He hardly moved a muscle and stood there quietly with his arms folded. When he wanted to say no, he shook his head slightly. When he wanted to agree, he nodded. He didn't waste a single movement, even to gesture while speaking! Everything about this man was calm, simple, and clear. Unfortunately, Hans didn't speak our language, and my uncle didn't speak Icelandic. But Hans did speak some Danish, which my uncle spoke quite well. So they were able to talk to each other without much trouble.

Soon I learned that Hans was a duck hunter—or, more exactly, a down hunter: He gathered the soft feathers shed by eider ducks, which can be sold for a nice profit.

When it came time to discuss a fee, my uncle agreed to pay Hans a certain number of Icelandic dollars every Saturday night. Hans would serve us as long as my uncle needed him. When my uncle stopped paying, Hans would stop working.

After they shook hands, my uncle offered to give Hans his first payment right away. But the hunter refused with a single word: *"Efter."*

"A splendid fellow!" my uncle exclaimed. "He has no idea of the historic role he is about to play!"

"So he's going with us to Mount Sneffels?" I asked.

"Yes," answered my uncle, "and then to the center of the earth!"

Now that our team was complete, it was time to pack the supplies we'd need for the journey. The instruments we packed included:

1. A thermometer, which measures temperature
2. A clock
3. Two compasses, which show direction
4. A chronometer, which determines distance
5. A barometer, which measures air pressure, and determines height above sea level and changes in the weather
6. A pair of Ruhmkorf's coils, which provide light

At the time Verne was writing A JOURNEY TO THE CENTER OF THE EARTH, a German scientist named Ruhmkorf was in fact working on coils that could use electricity to create light. But Verne is using his imagination here. He has his characters use the coils as portable lights and this is all before flashlights had been invented.

Among the tools we packed were pickaxes, crowbars, poles, hammers, and a huge roll of strong rope. We brought rifles and gunpowder too (though I couldn't imagine that my uncle really expected to find wild beasts underground!). We brought a pack of medical supplies along as well, such as bandages, rubbing alcohol, and various medicines.

For food, we packed enough meat and biscuits to last six months. We brought little water. My uncle was certain we'd find plenty of underground lakes.

On the morning of our departure, I awoke at dawn to the neighing of horses. Outside the window, I saw Hans strapping our bags to their sides.

I dressed. I washed. And then it was time.

As we said good-bye to Mister Fridriksson I was surprised to find myself feeling suddenly very fond of him. And then I realized why. It was probably the last time we would see him—or anyone else—ever again!

Kind of makes you wonder why Axel is still following his uncle, doesn't it? But as scared as he may be, I'll bet Axel is also really curious about what could lie at the center of the earth. So am I. Turn the page and let's find out!

5
Approaching the Giant

Maybe it was because the air was crisp and cool. Maybe it was because I enjoy riding horseback. Whatever the reason, as we set out for Sneffels, I found myself looking forward to the journey! "After all," I thought, "we're just going to hike cross-country, climb a mountain, and visit the inside of a volcano. This business about tunnels leading to the center of the earth is nonsense, I'm sure!"

Hans led the way on foot as uncle and I followed on horseback. The horses seemed to know the way by themselves. They trotted around crags of rock that poked up from the ground. They waded patiently through muddy streams. They moved at a slow and steady pace. Not even my impatient uncle could get them to speed up.

For almost a week, we made our way across Iceland toward that grand towering giant, Mount Sneffels. The farther north we got, the more barren the scenery became. As we approached the foot of Sneffels the ground became less marshy and more solid. Soon we found ourselves walking on sturdy rock. I quickly realized that this rigid ground surrounding Sneffels for miles in all directions was dried lava. **Mount Sneffels is a volcano that erupted centuries ago. The lava that came gushing out formed the solid rock they are now standing on.**

A spectacular sight that caught my eye was the geysers. These streams of hot water and steam spurted up into the air through cracks in the lava. Like nature's warning signs, they were scattered around the foot of the mountain.

But nothing seemed to distract my uncle. His gaze stayed fixed on Sneffels, as if to say, "That is the giant I'm determined to conquer."

On June 20 we reached a small town at the foot of Sneffels. It was nearly ten o'clock at night, but it was still light out because when you're this far north, the sun hardly sets in summer. There are even nights when the sun doesn't set at all!

Axel's telling the truth! In far-north countries such as Iceland, the periods of darkness in summer get shorter and shorter until the sun doesn't set at all! Imagine all the fun you could have if you never had to go inside after dark!

Hans removed our bags from the horses and had the horses returned to the stable from which they had been hired. Then he led us to the local minister, who was able to put us up in his home for a small fee.

After being shown to my room, I sat on the bed, thinking. There was one problem I couldn't get out of my mind. "My uncle's reasoning is ridiculous!" I thought. "How does he 'know' Sneffels won't erupt? Because it hasn't erupted for six hundred years? So what! Suppose it hadn't erupted for seven hundred?

Or a thousand? How does that prove it won't erupt next month? Next week? Or in the next hour?"

I hurried to my uncle's room to discuss this question and found him looking very serious. To my surprise, he didn't interrupt me as I spoke. In fact, he listened with care and concern.

"Axel, my boy," he said quietly, "I have been thinking about exactly that matter."

Could it really be? Was he finally listening to the voice of reason? Was he really about to drop his crazy plan and let us go home?

"I have been considering that possibility for days now," he continued. "I've thought it over very carefully because I believe that safety is of the utmost importance."

"I couldn't agree with you more, Uncle!" I replied.

"I've come to a firm conclusion," he continued. "My conclusion is based on the behavior of those geysers that surround Sneffels."

My heart leaped for joy. I felt sure those blessed waterspouts had frightened some sense into my uncle!

"Before a volcano erupts," he explained, "tremendous pressure builds up underground. This pressure affects any underground fluids in a certain region. If pressure were building up beneath Sneffels, the steam in those geysers would be blasting away with greater and greater force. But as you can see, the geysers are spraying their steam into the air steadily and evenly. So clearly, no pressure is building beneath them."

"But Uncle—" I said in disbelief.

"Enough, my boy," he interrupted. "With those

peacefully spraying geysers, the earth itself is giving us the go-ahead. Nature commands us to continue. We have no choice but to obey."

My last hope of changing my uncle's mind had been shattered. The next morning, Hans, my uncle, and I obeyed nature's "command."

Axel's uncle is such a quick thinker. The guy could sell cat food to a collie!

6
The Shadow Knows

Axel is about to climb a mountain that's higher than six skyscrapers stacked on top of one another! Or two hundred houses piled on one another! Or FIFTEEN HUNDRED doghouses!

Mount Sneffels is about five thousand feet high. As I gazed up at the white dome of snow on top, I couldn't imagine that we would ever really get there.

We walked single file. Hans led the way as we trampled over gray rock and patches of grass. Ahead I could see huge craters sticking up over the higher parts of the mountain. As we climbed, I thought how horrible it must have been when Sneffels erupted. I was sure that those tons of lava must have been heated by a tremendous furnace burning inside the earth. So why, I wondered, were we heading for that furnace? In spite of my fears, I marched onward like a brave, doomed soldier.

The higher we got, the more difficult and dangerous the climb became. Stones broke loose under our feet, causing small avalanches. But nothing bothered Hans. He kept walking ahead as calmly as though he were strolling down a country road.

After about three hours, I was exhausted. But we'd hardly got over the base of the mountain! We stopped for a quick breakfast and moved on.

Now the gigantic mountain became so steep that it was impossible to climb straight up. We had to zigzag around, weaving our way. Often, my uncle had to reach back and give me a tug to help me.

We came to a wide field of slippery ice; it seemed impossible to cross. But as we moved to the side we found a series of rocks leading across the ice. Like a monster luring us toward its mouth, Sneffels was giving us a flight of stone steps to guide us over the ice!

By seven that night, we found ourselves outside a towering crater. We were now three thousand feet above sea level. At that height it's so cold that there's snow on the ground all year long—yes, even in June! Worse than the cold was the wind, which blew violently.

My uncle and I were ready to rest by the crater, but Hans shook his head. When my uncle asked why, Hans replied with a single word, *"Mistour."*

"Miss who?" I asked.

"Look there," my uncle answered.

On the plain below I saw a whirlwind of rock, sand, and dust rising up into the air. This fierce tornado, which the Icelandic people call a *mistour,* was sweeping across the mountain…right toward us!

A mistour is formed when wind swirls around and around in a circle faster and faster...sort of like when I chase my tail. Of course, a mistour is a lot more dangerous! It sends huge rocks flying in all directions, destroying everything in its path.

"Hastigt, hastigt!" Hans cried.

I didn't know what that word meant. But his gestures made it clear enough. He wanted us to hurry around to the back of the crater. Though we were already exhausted, we hurried.

About fifteen minutes later, that whirlwind of sand smashed against the side of the mountain—right where my uncle and I had wanted to rest! If not for

Hans, our bodies would have been ripped apart and scattered for miles in all directions!

Hans didn't think it was safe to sleep outside the cone. So we continued our journey—another five hours! After eleven that night, we finally reached the top of Sneffels.

My entire body ached. The change in air pressure made my ears pop. I was in a terrible mood as we climbed into the crater where we were going to spend the night.

Then I saw the midnight sun and was suddenly cheered. How lucky I was to be in Iceland on the day of the year when the sun really does shine at midnight! I watched the sun cast its pale rays upon towns that lay sleeping far below us. I'd heard that people come from around the world to see this magical, wondrous spectacle. Now I knew why!

My bed—a pile of rocks inside the crater— wasn't very comfortable. But after a day of climbing, I slept deeply.

The next morning I rose and took in the incredible view. The world below looked like a giant painting stretched out before me. Deep valleys cut across one another in all directions. The valleys were sprinkled with lakes that looked like little puddles, and the mighty rivers that bordered them looked no larger than streams. To the side, I saw rows of glaciers—huge masses of ice that reached across rows of mountaintops.

A strange, wonderful, majestic feeling took hold of me. I forgot who I was, or where I was, or what I was doing.

But I was quickly awakened from this dreamlike state when I heard Hans say, "Scartaris." There, off to the side, was the peak whose name was in the coded note. The shadow of this peak would help us find our way. At this moment, the shadow of Scartaris was nowhere near the crater at the top of Sneffels. But we didn't need it to point our way yet. There was only one way to go...straight down into the mouth of the crater.

The crater opening was about a half-mile wide and shaped like an upside-down cone. Though it didn't seem that it would be so difficult to climb down into the mouth of the volcano, I wasn't looking forward to it. *I'm climbing into the mouth of a cannon,* I thought to myself. "Let's just hope it's not loaded!"

Hans led us down into the crater. Rocks stuck out along the walls of the crater, and we used these as steps and handholds as we descended. When we chanced to step onto some that weren't solid enough to bear our weight, they would tumble into the bottom of the pit. As they hit bottom the echo of the crash resounded like thunder.

By afternoon, we reached the crater floor. When I looked up, I saw a circle of sky. Up in that circle, poking into the clouds, I saw the peak of Scartaris.

We were standing on a round plot of ground—the floor of the crater—about a couple of hundred feet wide. Along that floor were three shafts—like chimneys—through which Sneffels had blasted hot lava from deep inside the Earth.

My uncle looked around and suddenly shouted with joy. "Axel! Come look!" he called. He pointed to the wall, where I saw, etched in that familiar code, the name that was haunting my life: ARNE SAKNUSSEMM.

My uncle was thrilled to know we were on the right track. I would rather have been on a different track—one that led home! How I longed to see Gretchen's smile or taste one of our cook's omelets. Or rest on my own featherbed!

"Everything is falling into place!" my uncle cried, pointing at the three shafts. I had no idea what he was talking about...until I noticed a shadow. The shadow of Scartaris had entered the crater. As the sun moved through the sky the shadow moved across the floor.

Slowly...very slowly...it was inching along... toward the three shafts! This distant peak was about to tell us which of the three was the right one! We waited for minutes that felt like years, as the shadow crept across the floor.

Suddenly my uncle's joy turned to rage. The sky had clouded up! Rain clouds covered the sun! Scartaris' shadow was gone.

My uncle paced frantically. He pounded the crater walls. He commanded the clouds to move.

And they did! As though taking pity on my uncle's misery, the clouds parted just enough to let the sun's rays pour across the floor of our pit— except for a small section blocked by a single peak. The shadow of Scartaris was back, just in time to point to the middle shaft.

"There it is!" shouted my uncle. "There is our path to the center of the earth!"

And so, on the twenty-sixth of June, at 1:13 in the afternoon, about a month after we'd left home, we began our real journey.

Their trip from Hamburg to this shaft took them most of June. If the volcano doesn't behave itself, they're in for a very hot July!

7
Down to Business

Finally our adventurers are starting on their way down into the earth. What do you think they will find out down there? Ghosts? Goblins? All those dog bones I've lost?

So far, I had managed to avoid looking into the shaft we were about to enter. But now the time had come to face my fear. So I took a deep breath, crouched, crawled to the edge, and peered down.

Within seconds my teeth were chattering! The sides of the shaft went almost straight down. Below, there was nothing but darkness—like the blackness of a bottomless well!

My uncle began to discuss how we'd get down this shaft. I wondered how we'd ever get back up! I wanted to scream, or weep, or beg my uncle to give up this quest. If Hans weren't with us, I would have babbled like a baby. But with Hans there, waiting for his next instruction with total calmness, I felt ashamed of my fear. So I kept my horror a secret.

"Axel," my uncle said, "strap the sack of food to your back. Hans will take the sack of supplies. And I'll take this sack of fragile instruments."

"But what about the rest?" I asked, pointing to a pile of ropes and other bulky supplies.

"They're not fragile," my uncle replied. "They

can go down by themselves."

With that, he had Hans wrap the pile into a bundle and toss it over the edge of the shaft. I heard a whoosh of air as the bundle plunged down. And I heard stones being knocked loose from the sides of the walls. But I never heard the bundle land! How far down was it to the bottom?

"Now it's our turn," announced my uncle.

Hans wrapped our four-hundred-foot rope around a rock at the top, with half of the rope hanging down one side and half down the other. As we descended we held onto both halves of the rope. This way, after descending nearly two hundred feet, we could rest on a ledge as Hans yanked the rope down and attached it to another rock.

Hans went first, my uncle went next, and I followed. We made our way down through the darkness without speaking.

I hated to count on just the rope for my life, so I made my way by stepping on rocks that stuck out from the wall. I had to test each rock, putting my weight on it gradually. Sometimes one would snap off and plunge down before I put my full weight on it. So while testing rocks below me with my feet, I was careful to grip those above me with my hands.

After about an hour, we came to a large rock that jutted out from the wall of the shaft like a balcony. We rested here, and I got up my nerve to look down again. Still, I could see nothing but darkness!

As we continued to descend, the circle of sky above us got smaller and smaller. Three hours later, I looked down again...and still saw only darkness below!

It wasn't until we had been climbing down for ten hours that I believed this pit had a bottom. Now when rocks broke loose from the walls, if I listened carefully, I could hear them land with a faint thud! At this point, we had gone more than a mile into the shaft. A half hour later we finally reached ground, where our bags were waiting for us.

"Made it," my uncle announced.

"The center of the earth?" I asked.

"No, Axel," my uncle chuckled, "the bottom of the well."

For a moment, my heart was filled with hope. "It looks like this is as far as we can descend, doesn't it?"

"On the contrary," my uncle answered. "There's a tunnel over there to the right. We'll enter that tomorrow. For now, let's sleep."

I made a bed out of a bundle of supplies. Then I laid down on my back and looked up. The tall walls formed a kind of telescope, through which I peered at the tiny circle of sky. I saw a single twinkling star as I drifted off to sleep.

When we awoke the next morning, my uncle was in a merry mood. "Well, Axel," he chirped, "how did you like sleeping in real peace and quiet for a change, with no horses clomping around in the street, or carriage wheels creaking?"

"As far as I'm concerned," I answered, "there's something eerie about the silence down here."

"If I didn't know better, I'd think you were nervous!" he said. "But I can't believe you'd be worried already, when we haven't even gone an inch down into the earth."

"What are you talking about? We climbed all day and into the night!" I replied, baffled.

"We've only just now reached sea level," he explained. "That long shaft took us to the bottom of Sneffels. But now, as we enter that tunnel we begin our journey into the bowels of the earth."

How completely frustrated I felt. We'd climbed up a five-thousand-foot mountain, then climbed another five thousand feet down inside it. But we were not one inch closer to the center of the earth than we were when we arrived at the foot of Sneffels. Our destination was still five thousand miles away!

Don't lose hope, Axel. There's an old saying that a journey of a thousand miles begins with a single step. On second thought, since these guys have FIVE thousand miles to go...maybe they should begin with a major leap!

After a breakfast of biscuits and dried meat, we approached the tunnel. "Now, Axel," my uncle announced, "we are really about to take our first step into the earth...toward regions unknown by man. At this moment, our historic journey truly begins."

I took a long, last look at the sky. Would I ever see it again? Then I entered the tunnel.

There was no sunlight at all reaching into the tunnel. My uncle took out the Ruhmkorf coil lamps. He put one around his neck and gave the other to

Hans to carry. As the lamps came on, that gloomy tunnel was filled with light.

And what splendor I saw! The lava that rushed through this cavern centuries ago had coated the walls. It had hardened into all kinds of shapes. In some places, the lava stuck out like long fingers. In other places, it clung to the walls in solid bubbles. Crystals of glittering quartz lined the walls too. And hanging from the roof were droplets of rock so clear they looked like glass.

Oh, the colors! The shades of lava ranged from red to brown to yellow. Other rocks glowed in all the colors of the rainbow as the light passed through them. I thought I'd entered a genie's cave!

As we continued on through the tunnel over the course of the day, the sights became less interesting...and my legs became more tired!

At eight that night, my uncle finally gave the signal to stop. I opened the water bottle and noticed that our supply of water was more than half gone! And we hadn't seen a single one of those underground lakes my uncle said we'd find.

"We've still got enough water to last five days," my uncle assured me.

"But surely we won't have gone five thousand miles to the center of the earth—and back again—in five days!" I said.

"Of course not," my uncle calmly replied. "But I'm positive there are springs beneath the earth. When we find the first underground spring, we'll have enough to last us the rest of the journey."

"But when will that be?" I asked.

"When we get through this crust of lava," he answered. "How could springs possibly force their way through these solid stone walls?"

I shuddered as an awful thought occurred to me. It made me so frightened that I could barely say it aloud. I mustered just enough courage to mutter softly, "But what if this solid lava goes all the way to the center of the earth? Then, even if there are underground springs, the water would never reach us..."

My uncle didn't hear me. Or didn't want to hear me. He was excitedly checking from barometer to compass. "We are now deeper than the deepest mines on Earth," he announced. "We are six thousand feet below sea level...deeper than anyone now living has ever been!"

They're deeper than any living human or dog has ever been? WOW! They've only gone the first six thousand feet, or a little over a mile, of their five-thousand-mile journey down, and they're already making history!

8
Which Way Is Down?

The next day, we made our way through the tunnel until about noon, when Hans came to a sudden stop. Before us, the path split into four narrow tunnels, one to our left, one to our right, and two more in between.

With hardly a moment's thought, my uncle pointed to the tunnel on the right. He had no idea which path was correct. So why did he make this snap decision? I believe he did this for two reasons: First, he didn't want to appear uncertain to Hans, whose full trust my uncle needed. Second, if he paused to wonder, his pause might have lasted forever! There was absolutely no way of figuring which path was the right one!

At first this tunnel was wide, with a high, arching ceiling. But soon it became narrow. At times we actually had to crawl along like dogs. **What's wrong with that?**

By evening we had gone six miles south but less than one mile deeper into the earth. That night, as I lay down to sleep in the complete silence within that tunnel, I felt lucky. After all, when you're above the ground, you can't just lie down and go to sleep. But here, we had no reason to fear wild animals, or storms, or thieves. Sheltered from those dangers by a blanket of earth, we could sleep through the night in safety and peace.

The next morning, my thoughts weren't so pleasant. As we continued through the lava tunnel I began to notice that we didn't seem to be going down. It felt as if we were going up! After three hours of this climbing, I needed to stop to catch my breath.

"Tired already?" my uncle asked.

"I surely am tired, Uncle," I answered. "We've been climbing upward for hours!"

"Impossible!" he shot back.

Though I tried again to convince him, the man refused to consider this possibility. He wouldn't even wait while I caught my breath. I had to hurry along to keep up with him. The last thing I needed was to be left behind in this underground maze!

Soon the type of stone around us changed. The walls weren't lava any more, but brown rock. I recognized this to be sedimentary rock, made from sand that has hardened over the ages. Thousands of years ago, this layer of rock must have been the floor of a sea.

Minutes later, I found tiny shells pressed into the rock. These must have housed ancient sea animals. The tiny wiggly creatures that had lived in those shells were among the first living things on Earth.

This worried me. According to the laws of geology, over time one layer of earth piles up over another. The higher up a layer is, the more recently it was formed. The last layer we had passed through seemed to have been formed before there were living creatures on Earth. The layer we were now going through was formed more recently. We were getting higher, not lower! I pointed out my findings to my uncle. He wasn't even interested!

The next day, we had to start rationing our water. A few mouthfuls a day was all each of us was allowed. *They say dying of thirst is the most agonizing death of all,* I thought to myself. *I have no interest in finding out if 'they' are right!*

The next clues I found only increased my fear that we were going in the wrong direction. Embedded in the sandstone I saw the remains of a full-sized crab-like sea creature. This creature was too big for any of the shells we'd seen before. I felt as if I were watching evolution unfold before my eyes!

Clearly, the animals whose remains were in this layer of rock lived more recently than those whose shells we'd seen the day before. That meant this layer wasn't as old as the last one we'd come through. We were still moving upward!

I would have explained my reasoning to my uncle, but he had obviously realized this himself. He hurried ahead, desperately searching for a shaft that would lead us straight down.

On the following day, we came to a huge cavern. I touched the black walls. Then I studied the black smudge on my hand. Coal! Coal was formed from the remains of the first small creatures to live on land. In those days, Earth was a warm, moist planet. Though life had begun in the sea millions of years before, during this period the first tiny amphibians crawled onto land. It was the remains of these small amphibians I was touching.

I should have been excited about this cavern. I should have wanted to study every detail of this museum of ancient Earth. But now the sights only filled me with despair. Since this layer was less ancient than the last, we were still going up. The path my uncle had chosen wasn't leading us close to underground springs. It was leading us away from them. And my thirst was growing.

At lunch I didn't even want food. All I wanted was an extra mouthful of water. That night I was so thirsty I could hardly sleep.

The next day, we continued along through a tunnel that seemed to be fairly level. By afternoon the walls on either side of us seemed to be coming closer together. Then, at about six in the evening, we came face-to-face with a wall of solid rock. There was no going forward, or to the right, or to the left. Hans folded his arms and stood there. My uncle was silent.

No sign hung on that wall. But in our heads we all knew we were at a DEAD END.

"So much the better," my uncle said at last. "At least we know we're not on the road Saknussemm took. All we have to do now is go back to the spot where the four tunnels began and choose another."

"If we can make it back that far!" I cried.

"And what would stop us?" my uncle asked.

"Thirst! By tomorrow we'll be out of water!" I answered.

"Sounds to me like you're out of courage," my uncle replied. With that, he instructed Hans to turn around and begin the trek back. Since it had taken us five days to get to this dead end, it would take another five days to get back to the cavern where the four tunnels began.

At that moment, I would have traded a diamond mine for a glass of pure, cool water.

Is anybody else thirsty? Or is it just me?

9
Not a Drop!

**In this chapter something Axel feared would happen...
really does!**

As we started to retrace our steps, each of us dealt with the frustration differently. My uncle was furious at himself. But he kept all his fury bottled up inside. Hans marched ahead, calmly accepting our situation. And I...I was downright miserable. But I did have one comforting thought: If we failed this badly in the beginning, we would of course have to cancel the trip.

As I had predicted, we ran out of water on the first day.

On the next day, I became more exhausted than ever. More than once I fell down in my tracks. My uncle was always there to pull me to my feet. But I could tell that he was about to collapse too.

Finally, on the fifth day, crawling on our hands and knees, we arrived at the cavern where the tunnels met. I lay there like a log. Groans and sighs escaped from my parched, swollen lips. Then I fell into a deep sleep.

When I awoke, my uncle was holding me up in his arms. "Poor boy," he said. His eyes were wet with tears. I saw him take out his cup and hold it out to me, saying, "Drink."

Was I dreaming? I stared at the cup in awe.

"Drink, my boy," he repeated.

I grabbed the cup and gulped down the cool water. It was just a mouthful, but that mouthful gave me new life.

"This water is our very last," he said. "I kept it hidden away for you, saving it for this moment when I knew you'd need it most."

"Dear Uncle," I wept, "thank you."

Though my thirst wasn't exactly quenched, the swelling in my lips went down. And I had enough energy to speak.

"Well," I said, "I guess it's clear what we have to do. There's no water to be found. Our journey is over. Let's head back to the surface."

As I spoke my uncle kept looking away from me.

"Yes," I continued, "we'll just have to head back to Sneffels. May God give us the strength to get there quickly!"

My uncle stood there, not speaking. Finally he answered, "So, Axel, the water restored your energy. But it didn't restore your courage."

"Courage?" I shot back. "Isn't it obvious to you that we must turn back?"

"What!" he exclaimed. "When we're on the verge of success? Never! Never shall it be said that Professor Lidenbrock gave up!"

"Then we're all going to die," I cried out.

"No, Axel," he said, "the last thing in the world I want is for you to come to harm. You go back. Take Hans with you. I'll continue alone."

I didn't want to abandon my uncle. But I did want to survive. Instinct told me to leave. I begged my uncle to change his mind.

As my uncle and I argued, Hans stood there with his arms folded, patiently waiting for his next command. How I wished Hans would help me get my uncle to listen to reason. But on my own, I couldn't do it. I had no choice but to leave the poor stubborn man behind.

I approached Hans. I motioned that we should leave together. I motioned again and took his arm. He wouldn't move.

"Master," he said, nodding toward my uncle.

"He's not the master of your life!" I cried with a fury. "He's not paying you to die for him!"

I tried to drag Hans along, but it was no use.

"My good Axel, calm down," my uncle said. "Hans will never desert the mission. But I have some news that will cheer you. While you were asleep, I explored the tunnel to the left. I found that it goes down quickly, deep into the earth. I'm sure springs await us there. So I'm going to make you a promise. Remember the story of Christopher Columbus? After many weeks at sea, his men became afraid Columbus was leading them across an ocean that would never end. They threatened to mutiny if Columbus didn't turn back. But Columbus convinced his men to give him three more days to discover land. And the New World was discovered! All that I—the Columbus of the Underground—ask of you is one more day. If by the end of one day we haven't found water, I swear to you I'll give up the search and turn back."

I realized how hard it was for my uncle to make this pledge. I accepted. What else could I do?

"All right," I said. "But we'd better start right away...our hours are numbered!"

Traveling along the new path, we came upon various metals. The walls were lined with copper, platinum, and even traces of gold. As we passed, the light from our lamps made these treasures sparkle and glow.

Toward evening, the glittering stopped. Now the walls had more of a white tint. We were surrounded by granite, an incredibly strong rock.

Granite is strong, all right. It's holding up miles and miles of Earth above their heads!

By eight o'clock, there was still no sign of water. My pain was unbearable. I felt faint. Finally, my legs would go no farther. My knees shook. I cried out and fell to the ground.

My uncle turned and saw me. His face was twisted in pain. I heard the words "It's all over" escape from his lips as I passed out.

When I opened my eyes, I saw my uncle lying on the ground. *It's all over,* I thought to myself. "There are miles of solid Earth above us. The Earth is our prison. And our tomb."

I heard a sound. Footsteps. It was Hans walking away. *Don't abandon us, Hans!* I thought to myself. But then I noticed that he wasn't going back up toward the mouth of the tunnel. He was headed deeper into it. Could he have possibly found a clue that could lead him to water? I didn't dare hope.

For an hour I lie there, waiting. Finally I heard the footsteps return. Hans approached my uncle and put his hand on his shoulder.

"Well?" asked my uncle, sitting up suddenly.

"*Vatten,*" said Hans.

"Water? Water!" I cried out, waving my hands and clapping like a lunatic.

"Water," my uncle murmured.

We followed Hans downward, stumbling along. After about a half hour, I heard a faint roar. It sounded like a waterfall. It became louder as we proceeded. Then louder still. The sound seemed to come from behind the wall of granite to our left.

"There's a mighty river on the other side of that wall," my uncle proclaimed. I couldn't wait to reach this river—to taste it! But as we hurried ahead the sound became more faint.

Soon we realized something awful: The water was trapped on the other side of the thick wall of granite! Hans had never actually made it to the water!

My uncle and I sank down in despair. I looked up at Hans, and strangely enough, he smiled. He took up the lamp and searched along the wall, pressing his ear to it, listening carefully for a spot where the sound of the water was loudest.

Then he took the pickax and started to smash the rock at the spot he had found.

Of course, smashing the wall of an underground cavern is a dangerous thing to do! But we needed water so badly that we were willing to risk causing the whole tunnel to collapse on us.

Hans struck at the spot with calm, steady blows. He aimed with great care in order to make a hole only a few inches wide.

My uncle couldn't stand the wait. He grabbed a crowbar, ready to smash wildly at the rock. I grabbed the crowbar to restrain him when Hans' efforts paid off. A jet of water burst from the wall. With a hissing sound, it shot all the way across the tunnel!

We threw our faces into the water—and then yanked them away. It was burning hot! The boiling water filled the tunnel with steam. But as it formed puddles at our feet it quickly became cool enough to drink.

Where did this water come from? How did it get so hot? We didn't even care. We lapped it up like animals.

When our thirst was quenched, we stopped to rest. As we sat there, the water began to form a stream at our feet. "I propose we name this stream after the man who made it," my uncle said. So we called it the Hans River.

Hans didn't show any emotion when we named this body of water in his honor. He was already busy filling up our water bottles.

When he was finished I suggested we stop up the hole. But my uncle had a better idea.

"Let the water run!" my uncle urged. "The tremendous pressure with which it shoots tells me that there's much water above. Let's allow the stream to run its natural course down through the tunnel. As long as we move down the tunnel, the Hans River will be at our feet."

"So our water needs are taken care of," I exclaimed, "for the rest of the trip!"

"Exactly, my boy," my uncle chimed in.

"And since water was our only obstacle, nothing can stop us now," I observed. "So let's resume our journey at once!"

"Let's get some rest first, Nephew," my uncle advised.

In all the excitement, I'd forgotten that it was night. Refreshed and relaxed, we slept very well.

Wow! When you're in an unexplored land and you find something...you're really DISCOVERING it! I really like this going-where-no-man-has-ever-gone-before stuff!

10
Moving in Silence

**Our explorers find themselves "beneath the waves"...
in a whole new way!**

It was strange and wonderful to wake up the next morning and not be thirsty! After washing down breakfast with water from the Hans River, we continued on our way. Now I was completely confident that we'd reach our destination. Why shouldn't we, with such a talented team? My uncle was a brilliant leader. Hans was the perfect guide. And I was the world's most devoted nephew. How could we fail?

Our march led us through narrow tunnels that twisted in all directions. But whichever way they curved, as long as they led down, we had no cause to complain. With our trusty water source at our feet, I felt we could continue forever.

On our second day in the maze, we came upon the steepest shaft yet. It went down sharply, twisting around and around like a spiral staircase of rocks. My uncle was thrilled to be descending so quickly. I was nervous about walking down such a jagged staircase. Hans, as always, showed no emotion. He simply got down to business, fastening the rope to rock after rock so we could make our way safely.

For two days, we went down this spiral staircase.

It was so steep that we had to stop every fifteen minutes to rub our aching calves.

Finally, we came to a much more gentle slope. The path became comfortable, though a little unexciting. *What a shame there can't be any interesting scenery to look at,* I thought.

We moved along in this way for days with very little trouble. We felt strong. We were in perfect health. Our bag of medical supplies hadn't even been opened.

But then one day in mid-July while checking his compass, my uncle made some calculations that alarmed me. "It seems we're twenty-one miles below the surface," he said, "and we've gone one hundred and fifty miles southeast of Sneffels."

"We're not under Iceland any more!" I exclaimed.

"You're right, my boy," he answered with delight. "We're under the open sea."

Why did that scare me? What difference did it make that there was a mighty ocean over our heads? Why should it matter whether there were roaring waves above or towering mountains? Whatever was up there, it was resting on a solid granite roof. Safe beneath that roof, we continued to descend.

Three days later, on a Saturday, we came upon a wide cave. My uncle paid Hans his weekly fee and decided that the next day should be a day of rest.

I awoke on Sunday feeling totally calm. It didn't matter to me anymore that we couldn't see the sun or the stars or the moon. It didn't matter to me that there might be fierce sea storms way above our heads or warships blasting their cannons at one another. Deep in the Earth, everything was peaceful.

"We're fifty miles below the surface now," my uncle revealed. "Have you noticed anything strange about the temperature?"

They're fifty miles below the surface? That's only a small fraction of the five thousand miles they've got to go to reach the center. But it's about forty-nine miles deeper than anybody alive has ever gone... an achievement really worth barking about!

I hadn't noticed anything strange about the temperature. It was as cool and comfortable as one could possibly hope. But according to the Theory of Central Heat, by this point the temperature should have been over a thousand degrees!

"Ready to abandon that Central Heat theory you so adore?" gloated my uncle.

"But Uncle," I argued, "it may well be that the earth around us is getting hotter. I believe we're being protected from the heat by these granite walls. How else would you explain that hot water jet?"

"I'm not talking about the water jet," my uncle snapped back. "I'm talking about the fact that we're going straight to the center of the earth—without being burned to a crisp!"

My uncle had an answer for everything. I would never win an argument with him. But that didn't matter very much, because if the temperature did shoot up and become unbearable, nothing he said would matter. We would just have to turn back.

Axel's right about that. Even the brilliant Professor Lidenbrock couldn't win an argument with a wall of blazing flames!

During the two weeks that followed our day of rest, the tunnel sloped sharply down. We talked less and less each day. Eventually we became like our guide, silent. We spent whole days without speaking!

I hardly remember a thing from this period—except for one event I can never forget. It was on August 7. We were nearly a hundred miles below the surface. On that day, our course felt almost flat; we were hardly getting deeper at all. I had been walking in front, carrying one of the lamps so I could examine the walls now and then.

At one point I stopped, turned around, and realized I was alone. *I must have been walking too fast,* I thought. *Or maybe the others stopped to rest.*

I retraced my steps, walking back the way I'd come for twenty minutes or so. But there was no sign of my companions. I called out. My voice bounced all around the cavern. No one answered.

I started to shiver and sweat. "Stay calm," I said aloud to myself. "They have to be here somewhere."

I went back up the tunnel for at least a half hour. Every now and then I stopped to call out. The only voice I heard was my own.

I stood there, trying to think, to reason, to

figure out what to do. But I was so frightened, all my thoughts in my brain came crashing against one another.

I was in front, I kept telling myself. *So they must be behind me.* Then I began to wonder. "Had I really been in front? Was I sure?"

I took small comfort in one fact, however. Whether they were behind me or ahead of me, they had to be in the same tunnel…somewhere. As long as I stayed along the Hans River, I'd be fine.

I reached down for the friendly stream that was about to save my life for the second time. All I found on the ground was hard, dusty granite! I had left the path of the river. I was lost.

Lost! For Axel, an already dangerous journey has become even more so. And in this story there is no faithful canine companion to guide him back to safety.

11
Lost!

**Now keep your eyes and ears open.
Help is on the way!**

No words can describe my terror. I was buried alive. Doomed to the tortures of hunger and thirst.

I crawled madly about, feeling the ground for moisture. But it was dry. The stream was nowhere to be found.

I must have taken a wrong turn at a fork, I realized. *That's how I got separated from the river and my friends.*

I had to retrace my steps at all costs. But how? My feet hadn't made a single mark in the hard granite. My head throbbed as I tried to figure out what to do. When I tried to reason, I kept getting stuck on that awful word: Lost! Lost!! LOST!!!

As I stood there, paralyzed, I felt the weight of the hundred miles of earth above me...as though it was all crushing down on my poor shoulders!

I tried to calm myself by thinking of Hamburg... Uncle's house...Gretchen...Mister Fridriksson. But the whole world above me seemed unreal. If only that roof over my head would rip apart and I could leap the hundred miles up to safety!

I knelt to ask God for help. As I prayed I remembered my childhood.

Praying eased my mind. As I stood there I realized that in my panic I'd overlooked a comforting fact: I still had food and water enough to last for three days. If I could only find the river, I could refill my water and make my way back up to Sneffels.

But as I walked, whichever direction I chose, I couldn't find a single stone that looked familiar. I feared I was walking down an alley that would never lead to anyplace I'd been.

And I was right. I realized it when I came to a wall of solid rock. A dead end. With all my courage gone, I dropped to the hard ground. There was nothing to do but lie down and die.

One day my bones will be found, I thought. *Maybe in hundreds of years, scientists will base new theories on my fossil remains.*

A fossil is a trace a creature or plant left from long ago. Dinosaur bones are fossils. So are imprints of ancient plants left in rock. Finding a fossil would really thrill me. But BEING a fossil wouldn't be much fun at all!

And then, yet another cause for misery: In my frenzy, I'd bumped the lamp against a rock, breaking it. The lamp was flickering, about to burn out.

I watched the last shadows flash against the granite wall. The last rays of light I'd ever see! An instant later, I was in total darkness. On Earth, even during the gloomiest nights, there are always a few stray rays of light coming from somewhere. But down here, there wasn't a single ray to pierce the blackness...not the faintest hint of light.

I felt that I was blind. Madness seized me and I lost all control. I tried to rush out of this darkness, darting in one direction and then another. Unable to see, I bashed myself against rocks, howling in pain as I dashed around. I felt blood dripping from my forehead, trickling across my face, but still I kept running.

Finally, I sank to the ground and passed out.

When I awoke, my face was wet—not with the water of the Hans River—but with tears and blood. At once I remembered my situation. Never in human history had anyone been as completely alone as I. I didn't want to panic again so I decided to stop thinking. I sat there, leaning against the wall.

Just as I was about to pass out again, I heard something—a sudden distant blast. Had a boulder shaken loose somewhere? I listened again. The tunnel was so silent I could hear my heart beating. Suddenly I heard another sound. The vague echo of distant voices! I became overjoyed. Then frightened. Could the words I thought I heard be my own, echoing back? Had I been talking aloud all this time? I wondered.

But soon I was certain. Those voices weren't mine. One of them was speaking Danish! I sprang to my feet and cried aloud, "Help! I'm dying!"

I paused and waited for a response, but none came. Minutes passed. Had my voice become so weakened that my words would never reach my friends?

I sank to the ground again—and heard the voices once more! Only in that exact spot could I hear them. I began to understand that sound was traveling through these halls in a very specific path. I leaned right into the point where I could hear the voices, mustered my strength, and called out, "Uncle Lidenbrock."

I waited for an answer. Several seconds went by. Then I heard the answer!

"Axel, my boy, is that you?"

"Oh yes!" I shouted back.

Between each of my answers and the question that followed, I noticed a long pause.

"Where are you?"

"Lost!"

"And your lamp?"

"Out."

"But the stream?"

"Can't find it."

"Don't worry, we'll find you," my uncle reassured me.

"I'm getting weak," I pleaded. "I can hardly talk."

"Then rest," he answered. "How I feared I'd never find you, Axel. We searched up and down the river. Then we fired guns up and down the tunnel to let you know where we were."

"How far apart do you think we are, Uncle?" I asked.

"It should be easy enough to figure, with the help of my watch," he answered. "I'll call your name, noting the second the word leaves my lips. The instant my word reaches you, shout my name back."

When we did this, my uncle saw that it took forty seconds for a word to travel from him to me and back. We also knew that sound travels a quarter of a mile per second. So we calculated the distance. We were some five miles apart.

Five miles! Hearing my uncle's voice had calmed me. But the distance made me tremble once again. We were miles apart...and I was still alone in the dark.

When you're walking through a tunnel, your voice bounces around the walls, making an echo. It seems that Axel and his uncle have found a sort of natural tunnel in the rock. It twists around in all directions, allowing their voices to bounce for miles...and reach one another's ears!

"Don't panic," my uncle said. "Just move toward the sound of my voice. Find the tunnel from which it seems to come, and follow it. As we move toward one another our strange sound connection will be broken. But keep moving along the tunnel from which you first heard my words...and you'll soon find yourself among friends. Until then, good-bye!"

I walked slowly, carefully, toward the tunnel from which the sound had come. I found that I couldn't walk. The slope was too steep. I had to drag myself along.

77

Soon the way got so steep that nothing I did could keep me from sliding. I plunged, falling freely down a shaft. I grabbed wildly for the walls. In vain! There was nothing to hold onto. I was falling into a pit of darkness. Suddenly, something smacked against my head and I lost consciousness.

Smacked on the head? Boy! Just as Axel's about to be rescued from one dangerous situation, he tumbles into yet another! Making a historic journey is no picnic!

12
The Central Sea

I awoke to find myself lying on a pile of soft blankets. My uncle watched me, tears in his eyes. As my eyes opened he grabbed my hand and cried for joy, "You're alive!"

"Yes, I'm alive, Uncle," I whispered.

"My dear boy," he continued, hugging me, "you're saved!"

Hans was excited too. "*Good-dag!*" he said.

"Good day to you, too, Hans," I whispered slowly. "So, Uncle, tell me where we are and what day it is."

"It's Sunday night," he replied. "Your terrible ordeal lasted four days. But as for where we are and how you got here, we'll discuss it tomorrow. You're too weak now. Your forehead is covered with bandages. Sleep!"

The next morning, I awoke—or thought I did. The things I saw and heard were so surprising, I felt sure I was dreaming!

Below me, the silvery sand on which I lay glittered. The floor was decorated with stalagmites, long fingers of rock that reached up toward the roof of the cave. The stalagmites glittered too, in all the colors of the rainbow.

But what light caused this glittering? No torch

or lamp was anywhere to be seen. Even more strange was the sound I heard: a faint murmur. It sounded almost like waves rushing upon a seashore. I also seemed to hear the sigh of wind!

Yes, it had to be a dream. But as time passed the sounds and sights didn't go away. Had my uncle changed his mind and taken us back to the surface of the earth? Or had our path taken a strange turn and led us back up? Had our journey suddenly ended?

"Good morning, Axel," my uncle chirped. "You're looking much better!"

While I devoured my breakfast, my uncle explained what had happened. When I plunged straight down that dark shaft, my body shook loose a huge boulder. The boulder knocked me unconscious. But it also saved my life! I rode the boulder down the shaft as though it were a flying chariot! And when I landed, I was found by my uncle and Hans.

Nah, that can't be right. We're only half way through the book!

"It's a miracle you weren't killed," my uncle concluded. "From now on, let's all stick together!"

"Tell me, uncle," I begged, "are my arms and legs all working?"

"I'm sure they are," he answered.

"And my head?" I asked nervously.

"It's right where it should be," he replied. "Except for a couple of bruises, it's just fine."

"But I'm afraid it's not fine," I said. "I'm afraid that I'm hallucinating. Because I think I see daylight and hear wind and waves rushing upon a shore."

My uncle smiled. "I repeat, Axel," he said, "you're fine. It's the science of geology that is in trouble. Why is it in trouble? Because there are important facts about the makeup of the earth that geologists do not know. Although...all that will change upon our return."

What was he talking about? I begged him to explain. Instead of speaking, he simply pointed.

At first I couldn't see anything. It was too bright. I had to cover my eyes.

But as my eyes adjusted to the brightness I was baffled. I rubbed them and looked again. "The sea!" I yelped.

"Yes," my uncle said proudly, "the Central Sea. In ancient times, people called the sea between Europe, Africa, and the Middle East the Mediterranean. They chose that name because Mediterranean means middle of the world. They thought their region was all there was to the world, so the Mediterranean was the sea in the middle of the world. But I have discovered the sea that really does lie right in the middle of the world. That's why I have named it the Central Sea."

The body of water about which he spoke extended as far as my eyes could see. At the least, it was a very large lake, if not an actual sea. It certainly had waves like a sea.

Where did the light come from? It wasn't sunlight. It had a duller quality. It didn't shine like sunlight—it glowed. This light was also different from sunlight in another way: It didn't seem to give off any warmth.

As I watched the sky above the sea I began to understand the source of this light. The roof of this great cavern above the sea was several miles high. Beneath it, thick clouds of gases swirled, constantly moving. The clouds crackled with sparks of electricity that caused them to glow. It was from these electrically charged clouds that the cold light poured.

So the earth isn't really a solid ball, I thought. *If this cavern is very large, it would be more correct to say the earth is hollow!*

How large was the cavern? I couldn't say. As I looked ahead on the horizon, a haze of gases blocked my view. But it was far larger than any cave I'd heard about on Earth. This was a world unto itself!

My uncle could see that the thrill of this discovery restored my strength. He led me along the shore to see what we would find. Countless underground streams flowed into the sea. When we saw the place where the Hans River joined it, I felt sad. "When we cross this sea," my uncle said, "we'll be leaving our friendly river behind."

Next we came upon another sight that made me wonder if I was dreaming again. Before us stood a huge forest. But the trees weren't like any I'd ever seen. They were stiff, gray, and shaped like umbrellas. There was something familiar about that shape. I couldn't put my finger on it—until my uncle coolly announced what they were: "Mushrooms!"

He was right! It was a forest of forty-foot-high mushrooms. Since light couldn't get through their massive tops, the forest was very dark and cold.

Beyond the mushrooms, we found even more amazing growths: Huge ferns as tall as pine trees! Blades of grass as tall as I!

"These plants are from a prehistoric period when giant plants thrived," my uncle explained. "It is as though we're visiting a greenhouse where ancient plants have been carefully preserved— except that this 'greenhouse' is as cold as the rays that give it light."

As thrilled as I was, for a moment I became nervous. Suppose animals appeared that were as large as the plants!

I was distracted from this thought by my uncle's voice shouting, "Bones!" Indeed, the ground was littered with gigantic bones, some as thick as tree trunks. **Did someone say giant bones?**

"This is the jawbone of a mastodon!" I cried as I

Helllooo!
Start flipping the
book pages and check
out the action....
Woo-cha!

recognized the jagged bone of that towering, prehistoric elephant. My uncle identified the bones of a dozen other mighty, ancient mammals that had lived and died on these shores.

Scientists who study prehistoric bones are called Paleontologists. They study bones to learn about creatures that lived long ago.

As we walked, my uncle came up with a theory to explain these underground treasures. "In certain ancient ages," he began, "violent earthquakes were much more common than they are today. I believe that a large section of the earth opened up. An entire region of the earth—and the animals that lived there— sank through the opening to this depth. When the surface closed over their heads, they survived and thrived in their new underground home."

Before this trip, if anyone had suggested such a theory, I would have thought him insane. But there we were, face-to-face with the evidence. In our hands we held the remains of ancient animals. Above our heads were the tops of ancient plants. And roaring in the background were the waves of an underground sea. Seeing is believing!

Reading is believing too...at least when Jules Verne has written the story. If this book had started out in an underground world with towering mushrooms and an indoor ocean, it wouldn't feel very believable. But by leading us here step-by-step, and by making each step seem realistic, Verne had taken us to a land you see in your imagination. Neat trick, huh?

13
Something Fishy

As we headed out of the forest, I was suddenly struck by something my uncle had said. Didn't he tell me that we were to cross the Central Sea? How? By swimming?

My question was answered before I could ask it. For there by the shore was Hans, completing a raft. While we'd been exploring, he'd been hard at work, making use of the tools we'd carried all this way. He had chopped old trees, cut their trunks into boards, and built a sailboat with a sail made from a blanket.

When we took to the waves, I learned that Hans had yet another talent. He was as skilled a sailor as he was a duck hunter! With confidence, he steered us across the water toward the unknown region on the other side.

"So, Axel," my uncle asked, "what should we name the port from which we departed?"

I thought for a moment. The face of my sweetheart came to mind. I answered, "The words 'Port Gretchen' would look good on a map."

"Port Gretchen it is," proclaimed my uncle with a smile.

The winds blew across this ocean with surprising power. After an hour my uncle figured that we had traveled nearly twenty miles! At that rate, he expected that we would cross the water in no time.

But when the shore of Port Gretchen faded from view, no new shore became visible ahead of us. In fact, I could see nothing but sea in any direction. Huge dark clouds cast their shadows across the surface. Silver rays of electric light reflected here and there, making the water sparkle. That was all there was to see.

After several hours, I started to notice seaweed collecting on the sides of the raft. As little else changed, it was only the increasing amount of seaweed that told me we'd been sailing all day.

We had a late dinner and then went to sleep. Hans stayed at the tiller as the raft rose and fell with the waves. Since the wind was steady, all he had to do was keep his oar still.

As the days passed, the weather at sea was superb. On one particularly calm day, Hans decided to do a little fishing. He put a bit of meat on the end of his line and tossed it into the water.

I had hoped he'd find some trace of life down there. So I was upset when hours went by with no results.

But then, suddenly...a tug! Something was tugging hard at that piece of meat.

"It's a fish!" my uncle cried as Hans calmly pulled in his catch.

"It looks like a small sturgeon to me," I said.

My uncle studied the fish with great care, noting every scale. It had a flat head and a round body, with fins sprouting from its sides. It had no teeth at all.

"This is no sturgeon, my boy," my uncle

concluded. "This fish belongs to a species that has been extinct for ages. A few traces of its relatives' bones have been found. But no human being has ever seen a fish of this kind alive."

"How can you tell, Uncle?" I asked.

"Its scales," he explained, "are of quite a unique shape and color. But there's something even more remarkable about this creature."

"What's that?" I wondered.

"It's blind," was his answer. "It has no eyes."

As I examined this odd fish, my uncle put another piece of bait on the hook. And another. And another. Each time, he pulled in a different type of eyeless, extinct fish. This sea was filled with animals that we thought had died out long ago!

"Could there possibly be dinosaurs?" I wondered. "After all, they were thought to be extinct too. Down here, you never know!" I took the telescope and scanned the horizon. But no, there were no living creatures above the water in any direction. And a dinosaur shouldn't be too hard to spot!

I scanned the surface of the sea, then turned my gaze upward. Why couldn't a pterodactyl, that huge prehistoric flying reptile, suddenly come swooping overhead? I'd seen pictures of the bones of one of these creatures, which a geologist had recently found and arranged. Nervously, I wondered whether I wouldn't see a live one right now, flapping his tremendous wings. With all those fish below, he would have plenty to eat. I gazed for a long time, but didn't spot a trace of flying reptiles.

I began to daydream. I looked out over the water and imagined I saw ancient turtles as big as islands. Across the shores passed a ghostly row of ancient mammals. In my mind, all the extinct beasts I'd ever heard of seemed to march before me! A towering, long-haired mastodon twisted his gigantic trunk, smashing it against rocks until they turned to powder. A monstrous megatherium waved his razor sharp claws in the air and gave a spine-tingling roar. A third massive beast waited behind a pile of rocks, ready to pounce on the others. It was an anoplotherium—that strangest of mammals—part horse, part rhino, part camel, and part hippopotamus!

Up in the trees, the very first monkeys were swinging. And way overhead, pterodactyls flew.

As I dreamed I felt that I was watching the world drift back even earlier in time. Millions of years were passing in seconds! Before my eyes, the mammals disappeared. Then the pterodactyls. Then the turtles. Then all the ancient fish, and even the tiniest squiggly underwater creatures. I stood at the moment when life was about to begin.

"Have you gone mad, Axel?" my uncle called, grabbing my arm. I realized that Hans was holding tightly onto my other arm. My trance was so deep I hadn't even noticed I was about to fall off the raft.

"I had the most amazing dream, Uncle," I said.

"Well, my boy," my uncle barked, "you'd better not have any more dreams of that sort. You nearly fell into the sea!"

Axel is a great daydreamer, just like Verne himself.

14
Battle at Sea

As the days passed with no sight of land, my uncle began to brood. He would search the horizon through his telescope, check his compass, and then pace up and down in our small boat, muttering angrily before raising the telescope to search again.

I didn't see why he should be so annoyed. The weather was fine. The raft was moving swiftly. After all the exhausting stages of our trip, this part was going quite smoothly!

"You seem a little uneasy, Uncle," I told him, after he checked his telescope for the thousandth time.

"I'm not uneasy," he replied dryly. "Not in the least."

"Maybe I should have said impatient," I added.

"And not without good reason!" he snapped back.

"But we're going as fast as a raft can possibly go!" I remarked.

"So what," he answered. "I'm not worried about our speed. I'm worried about the size of the sea."

When we left Port Gretchen, my uncle figured

the Central Sea to be no more than a hundred miles wide. We'd gone three times that far without a trace of land.

"We're not getting deeper into the earth," my uncle exclaimed. "We're not making great discoveries. This is a complete waste of time. I didn't come all this way to take a vacation."

"There are bound to be more discoveries," I argued, "as long as we follow Saknussemm's route."

"But how do we know he ever crossed this sea?" my uncle asked. "I'm beginning to think we might have taken a wrong turn."

"Even if we did," I replied, "I have no regrets. It's worth the whole journey to see this magnificent underground ocean!"

It sounds as if Axel is getting excited about the journey. At first, it seemed that his uncle was dragging him along by the leash!

"I set out to reach the center of the earth," my uncle barked. "I have no interest in sightseeing!"

I decided to give up trying to cheer my uncle. At least I was having a pleasant time. Hans was doing fine too. As it was a Saturday, he asked for his salary and put it in his pocket.

But at noon the next day, there was cause for concern.

My uncle had tried to test the depth of the sea

several times. He did this by tying a crowbar to a rope and lowering it into the water. Though the rope was six hundred yards long, the crowbar never touched the bottom.

This time, as he pulled the crowbar up, it felt heavier than usual. He called Hans and me to help pull. When we finally got the crowbar up, we saw that the end of the bar had been crushed.

"Tander," Hans said.

"You mean teeth?" my uncle asked.

I couldn't take my eyes off the crowbar. My flesh turned cold. There was no doubt about it: The marks on the end were indeed made by teeth—big ones. What huge jaws the owner of those mighty fangs must have! Lurking below us was a monster with teeth and jaws strong enough to crush an iron crowbar!

Over the next couple of days, I kept my eyes fixed on the surface. I tried to remember everything I knew about ancient sea beasts. I especially wondered about the giant reptiles that had lived in the sea during the days of the dinosaurs. I had seen the bones of one of these monsters in a museum. No man had ever seen one alive. And who would want to!

On Monday, August 18, toward evening, the sea began to get rough. Was I imagining things? Or was the surface really lifting up, bulging, on the horizon?

The next day passed quietly. But not the night. I was awakened suddenly when the raft was lifted right out of the water and came smashing down. I shuddered to imagine what might have thrown us about with such a violent force.

"Did we hit a rock?" my uncle asked, waking with a start.

Hans pointed ahead to a huge black mass moving up and down. My nightmare had come true. "It's a sea monster!" I cried.

"Yes," my uncle shouted. "Look there! It's a huge, hideous sea lizard! And over there's another one—a crocodile with enormous jaws and rows of monstrous teeth!"

As the first two beasts sank below the waves, another appeared. "A whale! A whale!" shouted my uncle. "Look at her gigantic fins and that huge tower of water she shoots into the air!"

Two more columns of water shot way up and came crashing down to the sea. We stood still, frozen in terror, watching these sea beasts. Without a doubt, any one of them could have gulped down our ship in a single bite.

Of the three of us, only Hans was able to move a muscle. He grabbed the rudder and pulled it hard, trying to steer away from this trio of monsters. But as we turned we found ourselves headed right into another fat sea beast with bulging eyes—eyes that were staring right at us. We turned again and found ourselves facing a towering serpent that flicked its five-foot tongue wildly through the air.

We were trapped. The beasts moved toward the raft and circled around us. I picked up a rifle. But what good would a little ball of metal do against the monsters' thick, scaly skins? I dropped the rifle and howled in terror as the beasts began to close in—on one side, the crocodile; on the other, the serpent. For the moment, I supposed the others had all dived below and disappeared.

Suddenly, the nightmare took a strange twist. The two monsters charged right past our raft and attacked each other. It seemed as if all four beasts were battling—the serpent, the whale, the lizard, and the fat beast with the bulging eyes! But when I pointed them out to Hans, he shook his head.

"*Tva,*" he said, holding up two fingers.

"What?" I cried. "Only two? It can't be!"

"He's quite right," my uncle replied, studying the battle with his telescope. "The first of these monsters has the snout of a porpoise, the head of a lizard, and the teeth of an alligator. It's the great fish lizard, also known as the ichthyosaur."

"And the other?" I asked.

"The other is the terrible serpent with bulging eyes known as the sea crocodile, or plesiosaur."

Hans was right! There were only two! For the first time, human eyes were gazing on the great reptiles of the ancient ocean.

The ichthyosaur had flaming-red eyes, each bigger than a man's head. Though quick, this whale of the dinosaurs was also enormous—a hundred feet long. And vicious! His jaw had more than a hundred sharp teeth.

The mighty plesiosaur was the serpent with the long tongue that whipped through the air. It had

93

rows of twisting fins all along its sides. Its most incredible feature was its neck, as flexible as a swan's—but more than thirty feet long. When it lifted this twisting neck high into the air, the creature became a tower of furious flesh!

A quick glance at these beasts made it clear: They were far more powerful and ferocious than any I'd ever seen. And they were turning every bit of their brutal power against one another.

Mountains of water swelled up beneath us, tossing our raft about like a toy and soaking us.

Twenty times I was sure we'd be plunged beneath the waves. The beasts' deafening hisses echoed through the whole cavern and chilled us to the bone. When they seized each other in a tight grip, I couldn't tell one from the other. I remember thinking that one of these two would have to win...and then move on to us for its next challenge!

My heart raced as I watched their struggle—a more gripping battle had never been seen on Earth. One hour passed. Two hours. Three. Yet still, neither beast was victorious. Again and again they charged together, smashing one another with massive jaws, mighty throats, and bloody heads.

A few times the fight seemed to be moving away from us. But then the creatures would rise up closer to our raft than before. When they came especially close, we grabbed our guns. We realized our guns would be useless, but had no wish to go down without a fight.

Suddenly the ichthyosaur and the plesiosaur disappeared below the waves. Their dive caused a small tidal wave that nearly sucked us down. Several minutes passed. Was this the end?

Then, only a few dozen yards from our raft, out of the water came the head of the plesiosaur. The monster had been fatally wounded. Its long neck twisted and curled in agony, slapping the water like a whip. Then the horrid neck just wriggled, like a worm that has been cut in half. Soon it stopped twisting and just lay there, a mass on the surface of the waters that now were calm.

But where was the ichthyosaur? Resting in his lair under the sea? Or waiting to spring back to the surface to destroy us? We decided not to wait around to find out.

Good choice, guys. We're out of here. See you on the next page!

15
The Real Sea Monster

Luckily, the winds picked up and blew us swiftly away from the scene of the battle. The next day was calm and quiet...until we began to hear a faint roar in the distance. As the hours passed, the roar got slightly louder.

My first thought was that it was a waterfall. My uncle probably would have loved plunging down a tremendous waterfall, since it would move us closer to our destination. I, however, felt differently about that prospect.

When Hans climbed the mast to view the horizon, his eyes fixed on...something. He came down, stood beside us, and pointed.

My uncle took a telescope and peered ahead. "Yes, yes," he cried. "There it is."

"What?" I asked.

"A tremendous spurt of water rising out of the waves," he answered.

"Another sea monster!" I cried in alarm.

"Maybe," my uncle replied.

"Let's steer around it!" I insisted. "I've seen enough sea monsters for one trip!"

"Keep straight ahead," my uncle instructed Hans, who remained calm.

Was there no way to change my uncle's mind?

This creature was at least forty miles away. But we could already see water from his spout soaring into the sky! The beast must be unbelievably huge!

Soon I caught a glimpse of the creature. His long, black mountainous body was lying on top of the water like an island. He was at least four miles long!

As we approached, the beast stayed completely still, as though sleeping. The waves that broke across his back never moved him in the least. His waterspout rose to five hundred feet, making a continuous roaring sound as it blasted forth from the animal's back.

We moved closer. And closer. I panicked. Something in me snapped. For a moment I stopped caring about the journey or my uncle's wishes. I wouldn't get an inch closer to this sleeping giant. I took a knife and threatened to cut up the sail. I started calling my uncle a fool, a lunatic, and any other names that sprang to my lips in my crazed state.

Suddenly Hans pointed once again to the monster, saying, *"Holme!"*

"An island!" cried my uncle.

"An island!" I echoed, as relieved as I was embarrassed.

"But the waterspout?" I asked.

"Geyser," said Hans.

"Yes, of course, a geyser," my uncle said, laughing. "Geysers like this are common in Iceland."

I'd been wrong—thank goodness!

Now that I wasn't scared, I could appreciate the

majesty of the geyser. The tall plume of water glittered in the light. Sometimes it shot up with even more fury, causing its beautiful plume to tremble. As the droplets fell from its spray, they shimmered in all the colors of the rainbow.

Hans checked to make sure the raft was in good shape while my uncle and I explored the island. Its surface was a mixture of granite and sandstone that was extremely hot. When I put a thermometer into the geyser, I noted that the water was a hundred and sixty-three degrees! Would we come upon higher and higher temperatures as we continued on our journey? Only time would tell.

My uncle figured that we had traveled over eight hundred miles since leaving Port Gretchen. That put us some eighteen hundred miles from Iceland—exactly under England! Of course, before leaving the island, my uncle had to name it. I was very pleased with his choice: Axel Island.

A few hours later, when we had left Axel Island behind us, the weather changed suddenly. The clouds of gas sank down near the sea. They became darker and thicker, hanging before us like a curtain. Soon, masses of dark clouds lined the horizon. Though the sea was calm, I had a feeling it would change at any moment.

The air was filling with electricity. I could feel my hairs standing on end, as though I'd been attached to a battery. If one of the others touched me, I think he would have gotten a bad shock!

Then the wind slowed down...like a giant catching his breath. "I believe we're going to have bad weather," I told my uncle. He just shrugged his shoulders. "We're in for an awful storm!" I continued. "These clouds are getting thicker and lower, as if they're about to crush us!"

Everything became silent. The wind died, as though nature had quit breathing. The sail hung straight down. The raft stopped moving upon the sea, which had become as still as glass.

"Let's lower the sail," I pleaded.

"No," my uncle cried impatiently. "Let the storm sweep us where it will. Just so it blows us to a coast."

Axel wants the sail taken down so that when the storm hits, they won't get blown all around. A very reasonable request! But the professor doesn't seem the least bit afraid of what the storm might do to the ship. He'll face any storm, any monster, anything to reach his goal.

The storm hit. It came from every corner of the huge cavern. It raged from every direction. It roared. It screamed. It shrieked with glee, as though demons had been loosed upon us.

The raft rose high on huge waves and slammed back down into the water, over and over again. My uncle was thrown to the deck. I dragged myself toward him, to hold onto the rope he was clutching. When I saw his face, I was amazed to find him gazing at the wild spectacle with delight!

Hans never moved a muscle. His long hair blew all around his determined face as he held the rudder steady with all his might. The sail spread out and filled like a soap bubble about to burst. "Let it down!" I cried.

"Let it alone!" shouted my uncle. As he wished,

we rushed across the waves at incredible speeds.

Ahead, the wall of clouds ripped apart as the sea foamed like the mouth of a rabid dog. Thunder exploded in deafening claps, and I was nearly blinded by dazzling flashes of lightning. Lightning bolts crossed one another, hurled from every side. In their path, waves rose up toward us like fire-breathing monsters.

As the entire sea raged with crests of flame, hail began falling! A million pellets came smashing down, clattering as they smacked our boots and clanged against our weapons. I clung with all my might to the mast, which the roaring wind was bending like a reed.

Through the night the storm showed no sign of letting up. Thunder blasted constantly. Lightning continued to dart in all directions. I saw it strike at the cavern roof, bursting into balls of fire. I wondered if the entire cavern might come crashing in!

The noise of this storm was so loud that we couldn't hear each other speak a single word. If all the gunpowder in the world were exploding at once, I could not have heard it over the storm! We were battered about and nearly exhausted. Hans remained as usual.

The storm got worse as the days went by. We had to tie down all our supplies. Then we had to tie ourselves down to avoid being washed away. At times the raft plunged so low that we were actually under water. When we tried to speak, it was of no use. Even when we shouted right into one another's ears, the roar of the storm drowned out our words.

Toward the end of the storm's second day, a ball of fire leaped onto the edge of our raft. At once, the mast and sail were ripped from the boat and went soaring into the sky like a kite. We were frozen, actually shivered with terror. This ball of fire—half white, half blue, about the size of a ten-inch bomb— rolled all over our craft. When it landed on the barrel that held our gunpowder, I shuddered. But it rolled off toward Hans, who seemed to scare it away from him with a stare. When it rolled toward my uncle, he fell to his knees to avoid it.

Then the thing came toward me. I stood there, pale and trembling in the dazzling heat and light. The fireball spun around my feet as I tried to skip around it. The awful smell of its burning gas filled my throat and lungs. I felt as if I were about to choke.

Then all of a sudden, I found that I couldn't move my feet! I was glued to the spot! That ball of electricity had turned all the iron on board to magnets! The tools and weapons were clanging together. And the nails in my boots clung to a plate of iron that was wedged into the floor of the raft. I couldn't move.

The fireball started rolling toward me again. I sank to the ground and struggled with all my might to rip the iron plate from the floor. I fell to the side just as the blazing thing bounced past me and exploded into a blinding sheet of fire.

Then everything became dark. For a day, I could hardly see a thing. The storm continued, but there was almost no lightning. Still we sailed ahead at tremendous speed. As the hours went by I figured we had passed under England...and under the English Channel. Then under France. And probably under all of Europe!

A frightening noise startled us. It sounded like the sea breaking against rocks. We found ourselves and our raft flying through the air.

What did they hit? Another monster? And more important, where do they land?

16
Unsure Shore

We were flung onto a shore. Our raft came crashing onto the nearby rocks. I would have been tossed back into the boiling, churning water, if not for Hans. Somehow, he caught me and carried me to safety. Then he laid me down on the sand, where I found myself in the company of my uncle.

My uncle and I waited beneath an overhanging rock as Hans returned to the raft to search for our belongings. The rain kept pouring. Finally, exhausted and aching, I fell asleep.

When I awoke the next morning, the weather was superb. And so was my uncle's mood. "We made it, my boy!" was his joyous greeting.

"You mean," I dared to ask, "the center of the earth?"

"I mean the end of this dreaded sea," he answered. "Now we can resume our journey toward the center."

I followed my uncle to the beach, where we found to our amazement that Hans had managed to save most of our supplies. He stood among these items, arranging them neatly. My uncle was so moved by Hans' work, he could hardly speak. Time and again, Hans had returned to the sea, risking his life to save the things we needed most.

Though he'd been unable to recover our weapons, the keg of gunpowder was still intact. He had saved our tools. And our food, which we had stored with great care, had also survived the storm.

After breakfast, my uncle got to work trying to figure our position. He was to determine whether we were beneath our German home...or whether we had perhaps made it to somewhere beneath the Mediterranean Sea!

When he had finished calculating the number of miles we'd come, he was thrilled. Next, he took out the compass. If we had traveled due southeast, as he expected, then we would indeed be beneath the Mediterranean Sea.

But when my uncle glanced at the compass, he came to a dead stop. He held the compass right before his eyes. He shook it. He shook it again. He was crushed. Too disappointed to speak, he held the compass out to me. The needle pointed due north, to the shore, instead of south to the high seas—the direction we had expected it to point!

I examined the compass myself. It wasn't broken. It wasn't even scratched. No matter which way we turned the compass, it continued to point north. Could it be? During the storm, when we thought we were plowing straight across the sea, could we have been spun around without noticing?

There could be no doubt: Our raft had carried us right back to the shore we'd left! The terrors of that sea voyage had all been for nothing. Every hour on the raft had been a waste of time. We would have to start out all over again.

"So," my uncle said, gritting his teeth, "fate will torture me. The elements themselves have decided to beat me. Well, let them do their worst! Air, fire, and water combined cannot defeat the will of a man! I will not retreat. I will not yield. Let's see who will triumph, man or nature!"

Standing on a rock, shouting at the sky, my uncle seemed to think he was the hero of a great drama. I, on the other hand, was less interested in risking a tragic ending.

"Listen, Uncle," I said as calmly as I could, "there has to be some limit to ambition. Some things just can't be done by anybody. We're not prepared for another sea voyage. Trying to sail a thousand miles on a pile of twigs a second time is absolutely insane."

I reasoned with my uncle like this for ten minutes without being interrupted. Then I realized why he hadn't stopped me—he wasn't listening.

"To the raft!" he yelled in a hoarse voice.

I broke down and begged him to reconsider. But I was facing a will more stubborn than the storm.

Once again, the good soldier Hans performed his duty without a second thought. He began fixing up the raft, preparing it for another bout with the sea. To give Hans time to complete the repairs, my uncle decided we should wait until the next day to depart.

Meanwhile, my uncle and I explored the shore upon which we had landed. Clearly, it was a very different spot from Port Gretchen. There was much greater distance between the water and the large inland rocks. It would take at least a half hour to travel this distance.

As we walked along the coast we found our feet crushing shells of every shape and size. Among these were a few huge shells, fifteen feet in diameter, which must have belonged to turtles larger than any now living on Earth.

After about a mile, the shore became very bumpy. It seemed there must have been an earthquake here long ago, for all kinds of rocks were left in jagged heaps.

Soon we came upon a large field covered with bones. It was like a huge cemetery, where generation after generation of bones had been left. I looked ahead and saw that the bones seemed to go on forever— white heaps of them far into the distance, blending together like a sea.

Excellent! More bones!

We were walking across the whole history of animal life!

And every one of the creatures whose bones we found was extinct. An incredible museum crackled beneath our feet! My uncle's mouth fell open as he beheld this endless collection of priceless scientific treasures.

He darted around, leaping from one pile to the next. And then he froze. He stood completely still, panting loudly, his eyes staring straight ahead. He struggled to speak, until a few words spilled out from between his trembling lips.

"Axel!" his voiced quivered. "Axel, come quick! A human head!"

Whoa! A human head in a prehistoric bone yard? I believe our journey has taken an interesting twist.

17
What or Who?

**To help you understand why Axel and his uncle were so
excited by the discovery, you need to know what kind of
scientific discoveries were really taking place back then.
Axel talks about it now....**

Only a few years before we began our journey, a
French scientist named M. Boucher de Perthes
had dug up a strange jawbone. Since it was a
cross between a human jawbone and a monkey's,
de Perthes believed it belonged to an ancient
human. Soon, scientists across Europe began
digging up bones of similar creatures, along with
primitive tools. Many scientists agreed that these
remains were evidence of prehistoric humans who
lived hundreds of thousands of years ago, in the
days of the mastodon and mammoth.

This new theory was bold and shocking. Until
this time, it had been widely believed that the
human race was only a few thousand years old.
Many scientists doubted the new theory. They felt
that these strange bones belonged to a few peculiar
humans who lived only a few centuries ago. Still
other scientists felt the whole thing was a prank—
that the bones might be those of orangutans and
the tools could be children's toys.

But the human head my uncle had come upon could not be argued with. He hadn't found just a couple of odd bones. This was an entire head—teeth, hair, skin—that seemed to have been preserved by the strange soil on this coast. Though the head looked somewhat monkey-like, it was not a monkey. It was human. This grizzly creature was one of us.

In Verne's day, scientists were very excited about the new theory that explained where human beings came from: the Theory of Evolution. According to this theory, human beings didn't just appear on Earth all of a sudden. Instead, over hundreds of millions of years, they "evolved," or changed gradually, from other kinds of animals that resembled monkeys. Since the head Lidenbrock finds here is a human that resembles a monkey, it seems to support the Theory of Evolution.

● ● ● ● ● ●

I'd never seen my uncle stay quiet for so long. For a while we just stood there, gazing at this head that seemed to stare back at us with its hollow eyes.

After minutes of silence, my uncle sprang to life. Lost in joyous fantasy, he began to lecture, as though addressing his peers.

"Fellow scientists," he began, "I have the honor to present to you an ancient human being. I know that there are impostors around today, boasting that they have discovered giants or dragons or characters from ancient myths. I realize that my claim may sound just as incredible as theirs. But my situation is different from theirs in one crucial way. I have proof! Feast your eyes upon your ancestor. This is the body.

You can see it. You can touch it. It is not a skeleton. It is complete."

My uncle raised the head to reveal the entire body, which he displayed to his imaginary audience. With the energy of a true showman, he continued his lecture. "As you can see, it stands at about six feet tall, an average height for a human male. The skull is much like ours, with the same sort of cheekbones. The jaw sticks out at the same sort of angle as ours. The forehead does bulge slightly, but not nearly as much as an ape's. There can be no question—he is our relative."

"I believe," he continued, "that in the age when frequent earthquakes shook the globe, this man fell deep into the earth and was preserved. And how fortunate for us all that he was! For thanks to that disaster, we have before us a human being over a hundred thousand years old!"

When he finished his lecture, I burst into applause.

Drawn by a burning curiosity, we continued to explore the bone graveyard. Every step of the way, I expected to find some new, amazing discovery. We found other bodies, many of them in even better condition than the first! My uncle could hardly choose which to bring back!

As we searched I began to wonder: Had these ancient humans fallen into the Earth and died? Or could they have lived their lives, married, had children, and died down here, just like those who lived above? If ancient humans had lived down here, could they be living here still? So far, we'd seen only sea creatures alive below the surface of the earth. But how did we know there might not also be ancient humans wandering these shores? And if there were, how would they respond to their visitors from above?

For more than an hour, we marched onward across this thick bed of bones. The Central Sea was no longer in sight, but my uncle was so excited that he had no worry of getting lost.

Eventually we passed beyond the bones and found ourselves in a kind of tropical paradise. Here, there were no clouds of flashing vapor in the sky. But electrical fluid seemed to be everywhere, making the entire region glow.

We came to a forest. To our surprise, it wasn't the mushroom forest we'd found near Port Gretchen. It was a wild and glorious wonderland. Towering palms and thick masses of creeping plants covered a beautiful carpet of moss. Though they looked like plants I'd seen on earth's surface, there was one striking difference: None of them were green. They were a dull yellow-brown, like old paper.

As I looked ahead through a clearing in the forest, I thought I saw—no, I really did see—moving among the trees, immense creatures. Mastodons! Not fossils, but living prehistoric mammals! Those enormous elephants bellowed as they uprooted huge trees with their tusks. The daydream I'd had of seeing extinct animals was coming true!

My uncle and I were shocked and amazed. "Come," he said at last, "let's get a closer look."

"No!" I answered, pulling away when he took me by the arm. "We don't have a single weapon! What would we do in the middle of a herd of mastodons? Please, Uncle. No human can survive among those powerful monsters."

"No human?" said my uncle, suddenly whispering. "You're wrong, my boy. Look! Over there! Unless I'm mistaken, I see a human being just like us!"

He was right. No more than a quarter-mile away, leaning against the trunk of an enormous tree, was a human being watching over his herd of mastodons. This was no fossil. This was a living...human...giant! He was twelve feet tall. His head, as big as the head of a buffalo, was covered with a mane of matted hair. In his hand he held a stout branch that he used to guide his herd.

My uncle and I stood perfectly still. At any moment this giant might look over and see us as clearly as we were seeing him.

"Let's get out of here!" I cried to my uncle. For once, he didn't disagree. We turned and ran as fast as our legs could carry us. Fifteen minutes later, we paused to catch our breath, far from that towering shepherd.

Now that I think back over it, I don't know what to believe. Maybe what we really saw was a tall, slender ape or an ancient monkey above a shadowy stump. But a human being, twelve feet tall, living down below the earth? Whatever my eyes told me I saw, that image is simply too outrageous to be believed.

And what did Axel really see? It's all part of the mystery of Jules Verne's story. We might not know for sure what it was, but it's fun to imagine what it might have been. But wait! There is more to come!

18
The Dagger

**What this tale needs is another strange clue. And
I believe our heroes
are about to discover just that.**

W̲e returned to the shore
and continued our
exploration of the
coast. We saw cliffs. We saw caves. We
saw streams tumbling over jagged
rocks on their way to the sea. But we
never saw anything that reminded us of Port
Gretchen. At several points I expected to spot the
boulder that had carried me to safety or to see that
little port where Hans had built the raft. There was
no trace of these or of anything else that looked
familiar. If we had returned to the same shore, why
did it look so different?

"There can be no doubt," I insisted, "that the
storm didn't bring us back to the same shore from
which we departed."

"I'm beginning to come to the same
conclusion," my uncle said. "Look up and down the

sand in any direction. Not one of our footprints is anywhere to be seen!"

I scanned the ground and realized he was right. Not a single footprint had been left in the sand. But something else had....

"Look, Uncle!" I cried, rushing forward to pick up the gleaming object at my feet.

"A rusty dagger!" he observed. "Why in the world did you bring along such a useless old knife?"

"It's not mine," I answered. "I thought it was yours."

"I've never seen it before in my life," he insisted. "Hans must have dropped it."

I shook my head. I'd never seen Hans carrying it. "Then maybe it belonged to that giant shepherd we were just running from. But no—it's not made of materials primitive people could use, like stone or bronze. It's made of steel!"

Before I could finish my thought, my uncle cut me off. "I see it now, my boy!" he exclaimed. "This is a special kind of knife, used by Europeans in the 1500s to kill an enemy after he had been captured. It doesn't belong to you or me or Hans or anyone living down here beneath the earth."

"Are you sure, Uncle?" I asked.

"Look closely!" he continued. "Those bumps on the edge of the blade were caused by rusting. This blade wasn't made a year ago or a decade ago. It is several centuries old."

"But if it wasn't left by any of us," I asked, "or by anyone living down here, who left it?"

"A man," he revealed, "who, I suspect, had taken

it out to mark a path to the center of the earth. Let's look around and see if I'm not correct!"

We ran ahead alongside a wall of rock, searching for a marking of any kind. At last, under a huge overhanging rock, we found the entrance to a dark tunnel. There on the wall we saw two letters: A.S.

"Oh, Great Saknussemm," my uncle cried joyfully, "thank you for this clue! Thank you for taking such care to show others the secret path into our mighty globe! I'm certain that your initials are carved upon the very center of the earth. And I vow, here and now, to follow your footsteps to that very spot, where I shall sign my own initials below yours. To thank you for your greatness in being the first to make that journey, I now name the shore near this cave Cape Saknussemm."

Before this point in our journey, I had seen some shocking things. In fact, I had begun to wonder if anything could ever surprise me again. But when I saw those two letters, carved in the wall three hundred years ago, I stood frozen in amazement. My uncle was elated.

I was so stirred by my uncle's speech that I burned with excitement—and with confidence. I forgot all the dangers we had faced. I stopped fearing the dangers ahead. If someone else could make it to the center of the earth, we could do it too.

"Onward!" I bellowed, in a burst of enthusiasm.

In the beginning, Axel was desperate for an excuse to avoid the trip. Now he's charging ahead, more eager than his uncle.

On our way back to Hans and the raft, I began to think deep thoughts. "Do you realize, Uncle," I said, "how fate has helped us out?"

"I've felt that way all along," my uncle answered with a smile.

"Even that awful storm served to guide us to the right path," I continued. "If we had managed to cross the sea, we would have come to a dead end. But the sea drove us all the way back, right to Saknussemm's path!"

"You're right, Axel," he replied, "all is for the best. We'll leave this sea behind us and continue on. To reach the center of the earth, we still have about four thousand nine hundred miles left."

"That's all?" I asked in my excitement. I was now as caught up in our adventure as my uncle. "That distance is almost too little to speak about." I was overconfident and eager. But I wasn't very realistic!

After reuniting with Hans, we sailed our little raft over to the cave where Saknussemm had carved his name. I jumped ashore first and led the way inside.

Within minutes we found ourselves inside a tunnel with granite walls. No sooner had my uncle lit one of the lamps than we found the path blocked by a boulder.

Frustrated, I yelled at the rock. There was no getting around it on either side, or above it, or below it. It blocked our way completely.

I was furious. Nothing else in the world mattered to me now. Not Hamburg. Not Gretchen. Nothing but getting past that boulder.

"Think about Saknussemm!" I cried. "He would never have allowed a lump of rock to block his way."

"You're right," my uncle replied, examining it closely. "This boulder must have fallen in the last century or two. Only since the days of Saknussemm has this tunnel been blocked. So let us get to work, chipping away with pickaxes and crowbars."

"It's far too big to be broken up by those tiny tools," I insisted.

"What other choice do we have?" my uncle asked.

"Gunpowder!" I proclaimed. "Let's blow it up!"

After a moment's thought, my uncle approved my bold suggestion. We spent the afternoon chipping a hole in the rock, into which we planned to pour our gunpowder. About fifty pounds of powder would be needed to break up so huge a boulder. We had to make quite a large hole.

By midnight we had finished. We poured the powder in and a piece of rope served as the fuse.

"A single spark will blow the rock to bits!" I announced. "Let's do it at once, and be on our way."

"It's time to rest!" my uncle insisted. "The 'blowing to bits' will have to wait until morning."

Blowing up? You mean, like, explosion? Uh-oh. Did anyone bring earplugs?

19
Kaboom!

When I think of that day, I still shudder. It was the twenty-seventh of August...and it was the beginning of the end.

At six o'clock we were awake and ready. Eager as I was, I begged for the honor of lighting the fuse.

Our plan was this: After lighting the fuse, I'd join my uncle and Hans on the raft. In the ten minutes between lighting the fuse and the explosion, we would sail as far from the cave as possible.

When it was time to put the plan into action, my heart beat wildly. I opened the lantern and lit the fuse. I watched it sparkle and hiss for a moment, then I charged to the raft.

Hans pushed off with a pole to send us flying across the water. As we sailed away my uncle watched the time.

"Only five more minutes," he said. "Only four... only three..."

My pulse raced. "Only two..." he noted. "Only one more minute...and mountains of granite will crumble beneath the power of man!"

And then came the blast. The roar was deafening. But I was distracted from the noise by the other terrifying things that were happening all around me.

The walls of rock in front of us parted like

A chasm is a deep, steep opening.

curtains. Meanwhile, a huge hole was opening up in the floor ahead. A single gigantic wave hurled us upwards. Then we were cast down into the hole, which had opened up to become a wide chasm. Saknussemm's path had been cleared. But instead of climbing down gradually, we were plunging into it— and taking the whole sea with us!

For hours we fell, our little raft carried along by the racing water. Our lamp had been damaged during the explosion, and water spraying all around made it impossible to light a torch. I could hardly see our surroundings. It felt as though we were rushing almost straight down at over a hundred miles an hour.

Hours passed. I groped for our cargo but found that almost everything had been washed away or destroyed. Worst of all—could it be possible?—no food. I examined very carefully every inch of the raft, searching for even a scrap. All I found was a piece of meat and some biscuits—not enough to keep us alive for a day.

I hardly had time to think about the horrors of starving when suddenly our raft was doused with water. The three of us gripped one another tightly so we wouldn't be swept away. Yet, for a moment I wished I had been swept from this awful boat, for the entire raft—and each of us on board—was below water. Unable to breathe, I panicked.

Seconds later the water rushed away and we could breathe again. As we continued to fall I became so exhausted that I couldn't stay awake.

When I awoke after a few hours of grotesque nightmares, it seemed that we had come to a halt. The roaring of the waves beneath us had stopped.

"Do you realize what has happened?" my uncle asked. "We're going up now."

I reached out to touch the wall, and in an instant the flesh was nearly torn from my hand; we were climbing even more quickly than we had fallen.

My uncle was finally able to light a torch, and we saw that we were soaring up a narrow well. The waters of the Central Sea, having reached the bottom of the well, were now thrusting us up through this shaft. We sped upward so fast that I felt a popping in my ears.

I was petrified. "At some point, Uncle," I asked, "aren't we bound to come smashing into a granite roof?"

"Axel," he replied, "I do believe the situation is somewhat desperate. At any moment we might be killed. But at any moment, we might also be saved. So let's be ready for whatever may come."

I screamed, "But we're totally helpless!"

"No!" he answered. "Where there is life, there is hope. Now let us eat so that we can be strong enough to face either victory or death."

I was in no hurry to tell him the bad news. "Eat?" I asked.

"Yes, at once," he said, as he rubbed his shivering hands together. "I feel like a starving prisoner."

Hans shook his head slowly. I held out the little piece of meat that remained. My uncle stared in disbelief.

"Well," I said after a pause, "what do you think now? Do you still believe we have the slightest chance of survival?"

Things are looking grim for our traveling trio. What happens next? Read on.

20
All Is Not Lost

Looks as though Axel and his companions are moving up in the world. Literally! Trapped in an active volcano on a runaway raft with no brakes—could things get any worse? Probably.

I noticed that the air was getting warmer rather quickly as we continued to rise. Was this a result of the blaze of flames described in the Theory of Central Heat? If so, why were we feeling the heat only now, as we rose upward, when we hadn't felt it below?

I soon thought of an explanation: Until this point we had been protected from the central heat by granite. Perhaps the electricity that filled the air above the Central Sea also served to protect us from the heat. At any rate, it became clear at each passing moment that we weren't protected from the heat now!

"If we aren't drowned," I told my uncle, "or flattened to pancakes, and if we don't starve, I think we might be burned alive." My uncle just shrugged his shoulders and continued thinking whatever it was he was thinking.

Over the next hour, the temperature continued to rise. Finally, my uncle spoke.

"Well, Axel," he began, "we must keep up our

strength at all costs. Let us eat our remaining food now, so that when the time comes to act, we are strong enough to do so."

"You can't possibly mean to tell me, Uncle," I cried out in amazement, "that you haven't yet lost all hope?"

"Certainly not," he answered coolly. "All is not lost, as long as a man's heart has power to beat and his brain has power to reason."

With that, my uncle took the last slab of meat and the soggy biscuits and divided them three ways.

Things are at their worst. But even now, as the guys eat their last soggy meal, Professor Lidenbrock doesn't lose hope. You've got to admire the guy!

Each of us ate our last meal in his own way. My uncle ate eagerly. I ate sadly. Hans swallowed his portion calmly, as though this meal were no different from any other! Was there nothing that could make this man complain, as long as he got his weekly pay?

"Fortrafflig," Hans said with gusto, after finishing his last bite.

"Delicious, indeed," my uncle replied.

Now that I ate, I became aware of other things I was doing without. Most of all, I missed that beautiful house in Hamburg, far above our heads...and Martha, the cook...and especially my dear Gretchen. These people and places passed before me as in a dream.

While I was busy grieving, my uncle was busy studying. He held the torch near the wall so that he could examine the rock through which we were passing.

"We've risen from one layer of rock to another," he said. "This granite seems to have been formed more recently than the granite we saw before."

"What could he be suggesting?" I wondered.

"Could we possibly be nearing the outer crust of the earth?"

The temperature was becoming unbearable. I felt as if I was being bathed in fire. When I accidentally touched the wall, I screamed in pain—for it was burning hot. To cool my hand, I reached into the water and screamed again. "The water is boiling!" I cried.

That's two strikes, Axel. Try not to touch anything else.

My uncle seemed amazed by this fact. It seemed to make a kind of strange sense to him, as though he was fitting together the pieces of a puzzle.

I would have asked what he was thinking, but I was too shocked by the sound of explosions. Minute by minute, we heard more explosions. They increased in number and loudness until they sounded like a single continuous thunder. I felt certain that the walls around us were about to come crashing together and smash us.

"What are you so worried about?" my uncle asked me in a calm manner.

"What am I worried about?" I yelled. "Don't you see that the walls of this shaft are shaking? Don't you feel the heat? Isn't it clear that we're right in the middle of an earthquake?"

"Not an earthquake," he answered, smiling.

"An eruption."

"An eruption?" I gasped. "You mean we're in the shaft of a volcano that's about to erupt? We're about to be spit out from the earth in a blast of flame and hot lava?"

"Yes," he answered calmly. "This volcano is our only chance ever to escape into the light of day."

As the hours passed I could see that my uncle was right. The boiling water below us, mixed with a heaving mass of lava, was lifting us up.

I realized that when we reached the mouth of the volcano, those rocks would blast in all directions and rip us apart—if the lava hadn't already boiled us. Yet even though I had no hope of surviving, I found comfort in one fact: The compass continued to show that we were moving north. At least before dying, I would be treated to the cool air of some northern land. Perhaps it would be Sweden or Siberia or Canada—or even the North Pole.

Toward morning the force thrusting us up became even more powerful. Above us, we could see the dim light of day. I was able to make out details of the walls of our tunnel. From these awful walls sparks flashed, hot vapors poured, and tongues of fire leaped out as if to lap us up.

Near the top, the temperature soared to nearly two hundred degrees. Sweat dripped from my every pore. If not for the breeze caused by our rapid climb, we would have burned up. Still we soared upward, faster and faster. At any moment I expected to be blasted out of the earth in a stream of flame that would burn us to ashes in an instant.

Suddenly we stopped. Our raft became completely still. The lava beneath us was no longer rising.

"Won't there be an eruption?" I asked.

"I'm sure there will be one, my boy," my uncle answered. "Lava sometimes approaches the surface of the earth in a kind of rhythm. We should be thrust upward again in about ten minutes."

He was right. Time and again our upward motion stopped, like a worker catching his breath, then resumed with full power.

During the pauses in our motion, I became so hot that I felt like I was breathing fire. The only thing that kept me alive was the belief that I was about to land in a region of subzero temperatures.

And then came the end. My memory of the moment is hazy. The deafening explosions, the shaking of the walls, the raft spinning around like a top, the falling clouds of cinders, the huge flames wrapping around us, the blasts of fiery wind that seemed to come from deep in the earth....

The last thing I remember is seeing Hans swallowed up in a blanket of flame, and having the feeling that I was flying out of a cannon as my limbs were being scattered through space.

Don't stop now! The fiery conclusion is just around the corner.

21
Journey's End

I must have been unconscious because the next thing I knew, Hans was holding onto my arm. I wasn't badly hurt, but I had been bruised in many places. I realized that I was lying near the edge of a cliff. By grabbing me just in time, Hans had once again saved my life. My uncle, who lay a few feet away, had also been saved by Hans.

"Where are we?" asked my uncle. Hans shrugged.

As my eyes adjusted to the light I looked around and was amazed. I expected to see snow-capped mountains and glaciers. I saw none. Instead, I saw bright rays of sunlight pouring across green hills.

The weather was warm! We stood there, half naked, and the sun seemed to greet us with its light and warmth. It was fine to behold the sun after two months underground. But we could have done without the warmth!

Clearly, we were not in an Arctic region. Where were we? At the foot of the mountain we could see a lovely sea, a little port, and a crowd of houses. There was also a forest of olive trees, fig trees, and vines full of grapes.

Just then, above our heads, a jet of flame shot up from a crater. "We should head down this mountain," my uncle observed, "or we will be injured by flying rocks."

We hurried down the slippery slope, taking care to avoid streams of hot lava and piles of ash. Along the way, my uncle snatched up our belongings, which had been scattered across the mountain.

When we came to the bottom, we found ourselves surrounded by fruit trees. Unable to control our hunger or thirst another moment, we plucked pomegranates, grapes, and olives as fast as we could. Then we found a spring of fresh water nearby, where we eagerly drank our fill.

> Great, now I'm thirsty again.

As we were washing our hands we saw a child spying on us from behind an olive tree. Though he was dressed in rags, we looked far worse than he. Our clothes were much more badly torn, and our hair was matted and scraggly. In fact, we were so horrid looking that when the boy caught sight of us, he began to run away!

After a brief chase, my uncle brought the youngster back to ask him where we were. In one language after another, my uncle asked the name of the mountain on which we had landed. But whatever language my uncle tried, the boy gave no answer. I began to wonder if he might be deaf.

Finally, my uncle tried asking his question in Italian, and the boy responded. "Stromboli!" he cried, and dashed off into the bushes.

"Stromboli! Stromboli!" I chanted. My uncle joined in, dancing as we sang these words together. We were on an island in the center of the Mediterranean! We had entered the earth in one volcano and come out through another, thousands of miles away! Our journey that had started in gray Iceland had finished beneath the blue sky of Sicily.

On our trip down the mountain toward town, we decided not to tell the townspeople how we arrived there. They would never believe us! Instead, we told them we were shipwrecked travelers.

"How did I blunder so badly in figuring our location?" my uncle kept muttering. "Again and again I calculated that we were moving north, when in fact we were moving south."

"I suppose," I said, "there are some things we just can't explain."

"A distinguished professor of geology," he insisted, "should be able to use a compass!"

As we reached the town, Hans asked to be paid for his thirteenth week of services. My uncle paid him and shook his hand warmly. For the first time in weeks, Hans smiled.

Local fisherman gave us clothes and food, then put us on a ship headed for France. After arriving there, we spent a week or so making our way northward across Europe.

Finally, on the evening of October 9, we

arrived in Hamburg. Martha was shocked that we were still alive. Gretchen cried tears of joy. **Home at last!**

"Now, Axel," she said, "you've really become a hero. So you have no excuse to leave me ever again!"

Because Martha was a gossip, news of our departure had already spread throughout Hamburg and around the world. People were amazed to learn that my uncle had returned in one piece. They were even more amazed when he described what we had seen—and presented one fossil after another as proof.

At a meeting of great scientists, he told the whole story of his adventures, leaving out only the confusion about our location. He ended by saying how sorry he was that we never did get to follow the Great Saknussemm's tracks to the center of the earth. But my uncle's modesty just made the other scientists respect him more.

Not long after our return, something happened that made my uncle quite sad. Hans decided to leave Hamburg, despite anything my uncle could say. The man was homesick!

"*Farvel,*" Hans said.

My uncle shook Hans' hand many times. Although Hans didn't display as much emotion as we, he did allow his feelings to show just a little: With the tips of two fingers, he gently pressed our hands...and then he smiled. I will never forget the brave duckhunter who saved our lives.

The story of our journey was translated and printed in many languages. It caused a stir all around the world. My uncle enjoyed the fame and fortune he richly deserved. You can even find his statue in wax museums!

In spite of his success, one thing continued to bother him: our error in figuring out our location. Then one day when he was working in his lab, I noticed the compass we had brought with us, and examined it. Suddenly, I whooped aloud. My uncle came running.

"What's the matter?" he cried.

"The compass!" I shouted. "Its needle points south, not north!"

"My dear boy, you must be dreaming," he insisted.

"I am not dreaming, Uncle," I said. "The poles are changed!"

When he saw that I was right, he was overjoyed. "I see it now!" He said, "By the time we reached Cape Saknussemm, the compass must have been reversed. So we really did cross the Central Sea after all! We really did pass beneath all of Europe! Cape Saknussemm really was beneath the Mediterranean, as I had predicted!"

"And I think I understand how the poles of the compass became reversed," I claimed. "During the storm, when that ball of fire magnetized our raft, it must have turned the compass topsy-turvy."

Pesty old fireball!

"Yes!" my uncle cried, with a loud, joyous laugh, "It was a trick of that strange electricity!"

About a month later, the Prince of Hamburg held a celebration in my uncle's honor. People from all over Germany came to get a look at the world-famous scientist.

The speeches were about to begin, and the town square was packed.

When the prince presented my uncle, the crowd went wild. People from one end of the square to the other screamed, cheered, and threw their caps into the air for Professor Lidenbrock, the bold scientist who had led our historic journey to the center of the earth.

• • • • • •

They made it! They went hundreds of miles below the earth, saw thrilling sights no one had ever seen before, and lived to tell the tale! And what a gripping tale it is!

Science has come a long way since Verne's day. We now know that no one could really go deep into the earth without burning up, since the center of the earth is about twelve thousand degrees (talk about Central Heat!). We also know more about the dinosaurs and prehistoric mammals than people did in Verne's day. If you check out a book about prehistoric animals, you'll find that some of Verne's descriptions of those beasts are not correct.

On the other hand, some of Verne's hunches were later proven to be accurate. He was right that our human ancestors' bones and tools would be found in caves. He was right that there was a lot of water below the surface of the earth. He was also right about uses that could be made of different types of electricity.

Verne's most important contribution to science, however, isn't any one specific discovery.

It's his whole way of looking at the unknown with his imagination.

The road to a great discovery begins with an imaginative guess. Verne himself wasn't a scientist or an explorer. But his imagined journeys pointed countless others toward real journeys that led to real discoveries. Among the people inspired by his books were the inventors of the submarine, the rocket, and the telegraph, and the first explorers to reach the North Pole, the South Pole, and outer space.

Even today, Verne's books are still inspiring people!

How about you? Do you think the book you just read might lead you to a bold quest? To try to figure out something about the way the universe works? To look for a way of solving a problem no one has ever thought of?

Could you make a great discovery? It might seem like a great deal to expect of yourself. But if you put your mind to it...who knows? After all, as the Great Professor Lidenbrock says, "Air, fire, and water combined cannot defeat the will of a man!" **Or a cute little dog. See ya!**